Murder in Venice

A LOTTIE SPRIGG MYSTERY BOOK 1

MARTHA BOND

ISBN 978-1-7396766-3-6

marthabond.com

Murder in Venice

Chapter One

'I'VE NEVER BEEN SO HUMILIATED,' said Mrs Moore. 'Or wet! If the rest of our stay in Venice is this bad, then get me back on the train this minute!'

Lottie Sprigg chewed her lip and wondered what she could say to improve her employer's mood. Nothing came to mind. Instead, the puddle on the marble floor grew larger as water dripped from Mrs Moore's turquoise coat, handbag and hat. The fox fur around her shoulders resembled an oversized, drowned rat.

Two maids hurried into the hotel room, each carrying a pile of towels. One set about mopping up the water while another dabbed at Mrs Moore.

'I should think I've caught typhoid now,' she continued. 'Or dysentery or some other awful disease you get from filthy water.'

'Hopefully not, you were only in the canal for a few seconds,' said Lottie. 'The gondolier pulled you out very quickly.'

'He's the reason I fell overboard in the first place! He wobbled his boat just as I was stepping out.'

1

'It was an accident.'

'It may have been an accident, but he wobbled it all the same. Gondoliers shouldn't wobble!'

The tumble into the canal had dampened their arrival in more ways than one. Until that point, Lottie had been marvelling at their surroundings. Stepping out of the railway station and being greeted by the Grand Canal had been like entering a painting of Venice she'd seen in a picture book. She'd sat in the gondola staring open-mouthed at the beauty of the cream and terracotta buildings. A domed church and ornate windows, pointed arches and little balconies and balustrades all gleaming in the sunshine. Everything looked like it had stood there for centuries, completely unchanged by the passage of time.

Their gondola journey had taken them along the busy thoroughfare of the Grand Canal, where other gondolas, water buses and delivery boats had battled for space. Then they'd turned into a narrow, quiet canal and moored at the Grand Hotel Splendore, where the water lapped at stone steps leading up to a little arched doorway. Lottie had been too captivated by the surroundings to pay much attention to the boat rocking.

The splash had broken the spell.

'Help!' Mrs Moore had spluttered, arms and handbag thrashing. The gondolier had stood astride the boat and steps and hauled her out. Mrs Moore - a wealthy American heiress - had been reduced to a sodden, bedraggled heap. As sorrowful as a limp fly which had just been fished out of someone's drink.

'I NEED to get out of these wet things before I catch my death,' said Mrs Moore. The maids began to bundle together all the wet towels.

'Would you like me to run you a bath?' asked Lottie.

'Yes please, although you could argue that I'm wet enough already.'

Lottie went into the bathroom and put the plug in the bathtub which stood in the centre of the room on four feet shaped like lion paws. Steam rose as she turned on the taps and hot water gushed into the tub. She found a pack of lavender bathing salts on a shelf by the sink and poured them into the water. The calming scent of lavender rose and tickled her nose. She wanted to get into the bath herself, but her employer's needs had to be seen to first.

Until a month ago, Lottie had been a maid at Fortescue Manor in the rolling hills of Shropshire, England. Her employer had been Lord Buckley-Phipps along with his wife and twelve children. During Lottie's five years at Fortescue Manor, Mrs Moore - sister of Lady Buckley-Phipps - had been a regular visitor. When she'd announced her plans for travel and the need for an assistant, Lady Buckley-Phipps had suggested Lottie.

Lottie had been elated at the prospect. Although she'd enjoyed her time at Fortescue Manor, it had been a fairly humdrum existence. She'd longed to explore the world she'd read about in books, and now - at nineteen years old - she had the opportunity.

Mrs Moore had spent a few weeks in London preparing for departure, and Lottie had joined her. In her free time, Lottie had hopped onto London's buses and trams and explored the city's busy streets, museums, galleries and parks. She'd also accompanied her employer to restaurants, shops and the theatre. London was noisy, smoky and grimy but Lottie had loved it.

ONCE THE BATH WAS READY, Lottie returned to Mrs Moore's bedroom and found a bellboy unloading countless suitcases from a luggage trolley. They had been brought to the hotel in a separate gondola.

The bellboy greeted Lottie in English. He was about the same age as her and wore a fitted red jacket with three columns of gold buttons. His flat red cap was secured beneath his chin with a strap, and his entire uniform was smartly trimmed in gold.

Lottie told Mrs Moore her bath was ready and began moving the cases into the simple maid's room. It was separated from her employer's brocade furnished boudoir by a little hallway.

The bellboy followed her. 'Just a moment,' she said, pointing at a battered case in his hand. 'I don't recognise that one.'

'It's not yours?' His brow furrowed.

'Is there a luggage label on it?'

'I can't see one.' His English impressed Lottie. Presumably he dealt with many tourists and could manage several languages.

'Is it locked?' she asked.

He laid the case flat on the floor. 'No. Let's have a look inside.'

He opened up the case to reveal a variety of gaudy blouses, skirts and dresses. Lottie pulled out a pair of lilac buckled shoes. 'I don't think these are Mrs Moore's,' she said. 'They're too big.'

'I apologise,' said the bellboy. 'I shall find the rightful owner.' He took the shoes from her, closed the case up again and took it back to the luggage trolley.

Lottie found her purse, which contained the money Mrs Moore had given her to tip hotel staff. She pulled out a ten centesimi coin and handed it to the bellboy.

'That's very generous of you, Signorina, thank you.' He

gave a grin which was handsome yet boyish. 'I hope Mrs Moore recovers soon.'

Lottie thanked him, and he went on his way. The maids had also left, taking the wet clothes with them to be dried. The puddle of canal water had gone, and Lottie smiled. All seemed well again.

She pushed open the tall shutters, letting in a blaze of midday sun. The balcony overlooked the Grand Canal and Lottie couldn't resist stepping out and taking in the view. Boats passed on the glistening water and the voices of the passengers carried on the warm breeze. The balcony had a wrought iron table with two chairs and terracotta pots of brightly coloured flowers. Lottie breathed in their sweet scent before stepping back into the room.

Mrs Moore's colossal bed had a carved mahogany head-board and gold embroidered eiderdown. To the right of the bed, two fringed chairs were placed at a round table with a bowl of cream carnations on it. A velvet chaise longue sat by the ornate fireplace and Lottie resisted the urge to rest on it after the long journey. Instead, she stepped over to the mirrored wardrobe doors and smoothed down her crumpled blouse and pleated skirt. Her brown bobbed hair desperately needed a comb through it. It had been difficult keeping up a groomed appearance on the overnight train from Paris.

'Lottie!' came Mrs Moore's voice from beyond the bath-room door. 'I can feel a headache coming on!' Lottie wondered how she could shout so loud if that were the case. 'I've run out of headache powders! Please can you fetch me some more? They must be Stark's. Nothing else will do!'

Chapter Two

'THEY NEED TO BE STARK'S,' Lottie told the man at the reception desk. He had oiled hair, sculpted cheekbones and a pout. The badge on his waistcoat said 'Lorenzo'.

'Stark's?'

'Stark's headache powders.'

Lorenzo pointed at the box he'd given her. 'Headache powders,' he said.

'Yes, I realise these are headache powders but they won't do for Mrs Moore, I'm afraid.' He raised his eyebrows, and she suspected he hadn't fully understood. 'Where's the nearest chemist?' she asked.

The eyebrows raised again.

'Chemist?' ventured Lottie. 'Pharmacy?'

'Farmacia?'

'Yes, that.'

Lorenzo picked up a pen and drew a map on a sheet of paper for her. Lottie thanked him, then made her way through the marbled lobby, zig-zagging around polished columns, well-dressed hotel guests, and large urns filled with extravagant floral displays.

The main entrance of the Grand Hotel Splendore opened out onto a piazza where tables and chairs were arranged outside cafes and restaurants. The sunlight was dazzling, and Lottie had to adjust the brim of her hat to shield her eyes. Following Lorenzo's map, she headed for the corner of the square by a pretty baroque church. She hadn't gone far when a tubby brown and white dog with short legs approached.

'Hello!' She patted the dog on the head and it wagged its tail. 'Or should I say ciao? You're an Italian dog, after all.' Lottie went on her way and entered a narrow, shady street. Barred and shuttered doorways lent it a mysterious air. The buildings rose four storeys high and washing lines were strung between them.

The street ended at a flight of steps leading up to a little stone bridge. Once she was on it, Lottie looked up and down the canal. It was lined with buildings of cream, yellow and pink, some hung with colourful flags and window boxes. A gondola passed beneath her, its long, plush interior furnished in gold, black and red. Its occupants were a young couple chatting excitedly, the lady holding onto the brim of her hat. The gondolier stood behind them in a striped top, dark trousers and straw hat. He steered the boat smoothly through the water with a long-handled oar and stooped down to pass beneath the next bridge. The feat required remarkable balance, and Lottie wondered how common it was for a gondolier to misjudge the height and either knock into a bridge or fall into the water altogether.

Lottie had fallen in love with Venice already. It seemed an enchanting, timeless place with higgledy-piggledy streets and canals and secretive little places to explore. She hoped that Mrs Moore chose to stay here for a while, but that depended on the movements of a man she had her eye on.

Prince Manfred of Bavaria was considered to be the most eligible bachelor in Europe and Mrs Moore intended to make him her fourth husband. This was the real reason for her travels, although she didn't freely admit it to strangers. Prince Manfred was known to travel widely and Mrs Moore hoped to bump into him at society events and make his acquaintance. The prince was currently rumoured to be in Venice which was why Mrs Moore had chosen this destination as the first stop on their travels.

Lottie consulted Lorenzo's map and continued her route. She passed a little shrine in an ancient wall and then a small garden with pink bougainvillea and large-leafed foliage creeping over the high walls. The balmy breeze carried strains of jazz music from a wireless or gramophone somewhere. Turning left then right, Lottie found herself in a busy shopping street. Small shops were crammed with all manner of things: books, shoes, bags, belts, paintings, hats, jewellery, glass ornaments and colourful carnival masks. Lottie wished she had some money to spend here.

Lottie followed the map as best she could, but felt she was gradually losing herself in a maze of streets. She felt envious of the people who had time to sit outside the bars and cafes with an espresso or a bright amber drink with slices of orange in it. She wondered what it was.

Eventually, she found the pharmacy with a green cross on its sign. It was a tiny place with a polished wood counter, shelves of shiny bottles, and a strong medicinal smell. Lottie was about to embark on her request when the white-coated pharmacist wagged a finger and appeared to scold her. The most repeated words were 'cane' and 'non'. And when he kept pointing behind her, she decided to turn around.

Sat behind her, tongue happily lolling from its mouth, was the dog which had greeted her in the piazza by the hotel.

'Oh, good grief! How did you get here?' She explained to the pharmacist that the dog wasn't hers but doubted that he understood. Then she took the dog's collar and attempted to lead it out through the door. The dog dug its paws in and refused to budge. Gently, Lottie then lifted the dog and discovered it was far heavier than she'd expected. It didn't appear to mind, though, and licked her face. 'Ugh, that's enough of that!' She carried the dog out of the shop and deposited it in the street. 'Now wait here,' she instructed. 'Don't move at all! I need to take you back to the piazza. Your owner will be worrying about you.'

Back in the shop, she was relieved to discover the pharmacist had heard of Stark's headache powders and had them in stock. Now Lottie had to worry about getting the dog to follow her back to the square. In a protracted conversation of broken Italian and English, she procured a length of string from the pharmacist. She went out into the street and tied it to the dog's collar.

'Well done for waiting for me,' she said. The dog tried to lick her face again, but she dodged it this time. She spotted a bronze tag on the dog's collar and inspected it. 'Rosetta,' she said. 'Is that your name? It's a pretty name. I'm guessing it's a girl's name? Are you a lady dog?' Rosetta couldn't confirm this, so Lottie could only guess that it was so.

ROSETTA SEEMED happy to be walking with Lottie through the busy streets. But now she was on a makeshift lead, she wanted to sniff at everything in their path. Cafe signs, discarded cigarettes, suspicious puddles and several other dogs were all inspected. Lottie soon found it was taking much longer to walk back to the hotel than she'd planned.

And there was another problem. She was lost.

'Oh dear.' They stood at a crossroads. 'All the streets look the same.'

Rosetta moved to go left.

'No, I'm sure it's right here.'

Rosetta dug her paws in again.

'It's right,' repeated Lottie.

Rosetta looked up with her large brown eyes and Lottie found it difficult to argue with such an adorable face. 'Let's look at the map.' She searched her pockets and bag, then she searched them again. 'Oh drat. I must have dropped it!'

Lottie looked around her, and nothing seemed familiar. Or was it? She couldn't be sure. She had, however, heard tales of dogs finding their way home after getting lost. She decided to risk putting her faith in Rosetta. She was already growing attached to the happy, tubby, short-legged dog. 'Alright then,' she said to her, 'I'll let you choose the way.'

Rosetta walked on, pausing regularly to sniff. Lottie couldn't tug much on the string lead for fear it would snap. For a while, she wondered if she'd made a mistake letting the dog lead her. Then she could only hope that if they walked for long enough, they would eventually find the hotel again.

Lottie's hopes were boosted when they reached the bridge she'd stopped on over the canal. 'Oh, you clever dog! I think we're nearly there!'

A few moments later, they were back in the piazza where they'd first met. Lottie led the dog over to the cafe tables, hoping that Rosetta would spot her owner. But the dog sat down and looked up at her. 'Who do you belong to?' she asked, in the vain hope the dog might reply.

Lottie walked around the square, then tried speaking to some customers and waiters. Those that understood her couldn't help.

'Now I don't know what to do,' said Lottie. 'I was hoping you'd lead me back to your owner. If only you could talk! I need to go to the hotel now and give these headache powders to Mrs Moore. I can't imagine she's going to want a dog in the hotel room.'

Lottie could do little more than return to the hotel and

hope that Lorenzo, or another member of the hotel staff, could help.

They stepped into the grand lobby and had walked only three paces before a man in a dark suit rushed at them and bundled the dog into his arms.

'Rosetta!' He buried his face into the dog's fur and poured out a torrent of words which Lottie could only guess expressed joy and relief. Then he got to his feet, seized Lottie's hand, and pumped her arm firmly up and down while expressing more loud words of gratitude.

'It's quite alright,' said Lottie demurely, a little embarrassed by the glances they were now receiving from the other guests in the lobby.

'Oh! English? Thank you! Thank you very much! You saved my life!'

He was a short man and aged about fifty. His hair looked artificially dark and a strong jawline was softened by jowls that wobbled as he talked. He was smartly dressed, but his shirt buttons strained at the belly. Each of his fingers bore a ring and the top buttons of his shirt were undone to show off a gold necklace.

'I found her in the piazza,' explained Lottie.

'You are wonderful! How can I ever repay you?'

'There's no need to. Rosetta followed me and all I did was attach some string to her collar and bring her back here.'

'I thought someone had snatched her. You have heard about the dog snatcher?'

'No. How horrible!'

'It is horrible indeed. When I saw she was gone, I thought the dog snatcher had taken her from beneath my very nose.' He pressed a thick forefinger on his nose to demonstrate. 'She's a Pembroke Welsh Corgi, you see. Dog snatchers like them a lot. I thought I would never see her again! Now you must be my guest this evening!'

'Guest?' Lottie needed to explain to him she was a lowly assistant and wasn't the sort of person to be invited anywhere.

'Yes, yes! I am performing in Don Giovanni tonight at the Teatro La Fenice. You will come to the opera and after that you will dine with me in this very hotel! It is how I wish to say thank you.'

Lottie explained her circumstances and told him she would need to get permission from her employer, Mrs Moore.

'And so Mrs Moore must come too! Tell her that Amadeo Moretti invites her and that he does not take no for an answer!'

Chapter Three

'He won't take no for an answer?' said Mrs Moore. She had finished her bath and now reclined on the chaise longue in a blue silk robe with a Japanese print on it. The headache appeared to have passed already. 'Who does he think he is?'

'He's an opera singer. Amadeo Moretti,' replied Lottie.

'Is he famous?'

'I don't know.'

'I need you to find out if he's famous. Ask the hotel manager, Signor Borelli, about him. Apparently he knows everyone. You'll find it easy to chat to him as you know a little Italian.'

'I don't know Italian.'

'Oh? I thought you did.'

'They taught us French at the orphanage.'

'French! I remember now. Very useful in France, but less useful in Italy.'

The telephone by the bed gave a shrill ring. Lottie answered it.

'Hello. Good afternoon. This is Lorenzo at the reception desk. There is a gentleman here with a gift for Mrs Moore.'

'Thank you.' Lottie replaced the receiver and repeated the message.

'Which gentleman?' asked Mrs Moore.

'He didn't say.'

'But I'm clearly in no state to be receiving visitors at the present time. You'll have to go down and see who it is.'

Lottie went on her way, intrigued to find out who it was and what the gift could be. She skipped down the wide steps of the grand staircase and spotted a gondolier at the reception desk holding a bunch of pink roses. As she approached, she recognised him as the gondolier who had pulled Mrs Moore out of the canal. He was a young man with dark, close-set eyes, a long nose and a long face. He removed his boater hat and gave a reverent bow as Lottie greeted him.

'My most humble apologies to Signora,' he said, handing Lottie the roses.

She enjoyed a sniff of their heady scent. 'Thank you, that's very kind of you. I'm sure there's no need for the gift, it was an accident.'

'It was careless of me. The last thing I want is one of my customers falling into the canal. It's a gondolier's nightmare. How is Signora?'

'She's very well and fully recovered.'

'I hope she will accept these flowers as a token of my regret.'

'Thank you again.'

He gave another bow, and Lottie wanted to tell him there was no need to be so humble about it all.

'A quick question, if I may?' she asked. 'Is Amadeo Moretti famous?'

'The singer?'

'You've heard of him? So he is famous?'

'Famous? Yes. He is here in Venice, singing at the opera! You should go and watch him.'

'Thank you. I will!'

'WELL, I suppose it's something when someone apologises,' said Mrs Moore, accepting the roses. 'It doesn't happen a great deal these days, does it? People don't like to admit they've made a mistake. These roses smell delightful, let's put them in some water in the bathroom sink for now.' She handed them back.

'Amadeo Moretti is famous,' said Lottie.

'Is he?' A smile grew on her lips.

'The gondolier has heard of him.'

'Well, that settles it then. Off to the opera it is.'

'What about your headache?'

'Oh, that went ages ago.' Mrs Moore picked up her lorgnette, which hung from her neck on a gold chain. She peered through the two lenses and looked Lottie up and down. 'What are you planning to wear to the opera this evening?'

'My blue dress.'

'Not the nautical one with the sailor's collar and bow?'

'Yes.'

'You can't wear that to the opera.'

'What can I wear then? Something of yours?'

Mrs Moore laughed. 'I'm significantly shorter and wider than you, Lottie. No, we shall have to ask that French lady we met on the train if she has anything to lend you. She looks about the same size.'

'Camille Lapointe?' Lottie felt intimidated by the beautiful writer. She was so elegant and well-educated that Lottie felt like an ungainly halfwit in comparison.

'Yes, I'm sure she won't mind lending you something. And whatever it is, it will be extremely fashionable I'm sure. Just ask to borrow one of her outfits. She's in room fourteen.'

'But I can't just ask her. I hardly know her.'

'We spent a day and a night on a train with her!'

'But she's a writer and I'm just a...'

'Go and ask, Lottie. You have nothing to lose. The very worst outcome is that she'll say no and we'll have to quickly have one of my dresses altered for you.'

LOTTIE MADE her way to room fourteen, dragging her feet. She practised posing the question, trying to make it sound polite.

She paused at room fourteen and took a breath to calm her nerves. Then she tentatively knocked and stepped back, hoping she could return to Mrs Moore and tell her there'd been no answer.

Madame Lapointe answered the door, silver cigarette holder in hand. 'Oui?' Her other hand was pushed into the pocket of a fashionable indigo woollen jacket, belted low at the waist. She wore it over a matching skirt which skimmed her knees. Her large eyes were edged with black and she had a delicate, porcelain face. Her dark hair was styled in a short, sharp bob.

Lottie explained, in flustering detail, that she needed a dress for the opera and Mrs Moore had sent her to ask about one.

Madame Lapointe inhaled on her cigarette and lazily blew out a cloud of smoke. 'I might have something. Wait here.'

The door was closed on Lottie as she waited in the corridor. A maid passed by with a trolley and Lottie gave her an uneasy wave. A few minutes later, the door opened a crack and a shiny silk dress was thrust out. It was magenta with a panel of gold gathered at the front in a low waist. The skirt was full and the hem fashionably asymmetrical. Lottie had never worn anything as beautiful as this before.

'Thank you so much!' she said.

'De rien,' came the reply from beyond the door before it was closed again.

'VERY STYLISH,' said Mrs Moore, checking the label. 'Chanel? I've not heard of that brand. I think I have some gloves in a similar pink, they'll match nicely. A headdress would look pretty too.'

Lottie got changed among the stacked-up suitcases in her little room. Once ready, she returned to Mrs Moore's room to look at herself in the wardrobe mirror.

'Beautiful!' said Mrs Moore. 'You scrub up very well indeed. You could pass for a lady!'

Lottie blushed and felt pleased with the young woman in the mirror. The dress fitted perfectly and looked remarkably glamorous once she put on the gloves, a necklace, and one of Mrs Moore's beaded headbands with a feather in it.

Mrs Moore was radiant in an emerald green satin floor-length gown and a colourful embroidered cape with a fur collar. She hadn't yet embraced the shorter hems and unfussy lines of modern clothes. Her wide-brimmed hat was a style worn before the war, but this didn't bother Mrs Moore. She had her own sense of fashion and stuck to it.

There was a knock at the door and Lottie feared Madame Lapointe had changed her mind about the dress and wanted it back. When she opened the door, the bellboy stood there. He raised his eyebrows, then his mouth opened and closed like a goldfish.

'Can I help?' Lottie asked, filling the silence. It seemed he'd been struck dumb by the drastic change in her appearance.

His cheeks reddened, and he handed her a glass vase. 'Lorenzo told me you need this for the flowers.'

'That's very thoughtful of Lorenzo. Thank you!'

The bellboy gave a nod, his eyes still fixed on her.

'Thank you then,' she said. 'Goodbye.'

'Yes.' He blinked, then shook his head as if coming to his senses. 'Ciao.'

'THAT'S VERY CONSIDERATE, but there's no need for the vase,' said Mrs Moore. 'We can take the flowers with us and give them to Amadeo Moretti as a token of our appreciation.'

'But the gondolier intended them to be a gift for you.'

'He's not going to find out we've given them to someone else, is he? Go and grab them from the bathroom and come along. We mustn't be late for the opera.'

Chapter Four

'How lovely to find a gondolier who doesn't throw you overboard,' said Mrs Moore as they disembarked by the opera house. The setting sun bathed the columned facade in golden light and a host of people in colourful finery climbed the steps to the main entrance. Lottie and Mrs Moore followed them.

In the ornate foyer, well-scented people thronged beneath an enormous chandelier. In her stylish dress, Lottie felt she could almost fit in here. She lifted her chin and attempted to project an air of good breeding.

'We need to find Amadeo Moretti's dressing room,' said Mrs Moore. 'I can't wait to meet him before he goes on stage. Please go and find someone to ask.'

Lottie went on her way, clutching the roses. She found a man in a smart, braided uniform and explained she had a gift for her good friend, Signor Moretti.

'He is a friend of yours?' The man looked her up and down.

'Yes. My employer and I are guests of his this evening. You

can ask him yourself. Just mention the name Lottie Sprigg and his dog Rosetta, and he will confirm it.'

'Lottie?'

'Sprigg.'

'Lottie Sprigg and Rosetta?'

'His dog is called Rosetta. I found her for him.'

'Wait here.'

Lottie did so as he disappeared through a door which was barely visible in the panelled wall.

'You'll have to see Amadeo Moretti alone.' Mrs Moore appeared at her side, slightly breathless.

'Why?'

'I've just heard word that Prince Manfred is here. Can you believe it?'

'Where?' Lottie glanced about for a glimpse of the infamous man.

'I don't know where yet.' She picked up her lorgnette and scanned the crowd through them. 'I'll find him. Pass on my regards to Signor Moretti and tell him I'll see him at dinner. Oh, and tell him to break a leg. Do they say that in opera like they do in theatre?'

'I don't know.'

'Well, say it anyway. It can't be bad luck, can it?'

'I hope not.'

As soon as Mrs Moore disappeared, the uniformed man reappeared. 'This way please, Signorina.'

She followed him through the door and down some steps to a stone corridor which was cold and spartan when compared to the grand foyer she'd just been waiting in.

They passed a red door with a name on it. Then another. Lottie guessed these were the dressing rooms for the cast and she anticipated they'd soon reach Amadeo Moretti's door. Up ahead, a lady in a low-waisted black lace dress stepped out and closed a door behind her. She walked in their direction, but swiftly turned as soon as she noticed them. She walked away from view, moving quickly.

The lady had only been there for a few seconds, but Lottie felt sure she recognised her.

Camille Lapointe.

Why hadn't she mentioned she was going to the opera too? And what was she doing here backstage?

Visiting Amadeo Moretti, it seemed. The door she had stepped out of was the door to his dressing room. The uniformed man gave a quick rap, and they went inside.

'Signorina Sprigg,' announced the uniformed man with a bow.

Amadeo Moretti sprang out of his seat at his dressing table and gave a bow. His opulent costume impressed Lottie. He wore a red and gold jacket with puffed up shoulders and large cuffs. A red silk cravat was tied into a bow beneath the wide ruffled collar of his shirt and he wore a shiny gold waistcoat over red breeches.

Lottie presented him with the flowers, noticing there were several other bunches already arranged in vases around the room. Despite this, he accepted them graciously. 'Mrs Moore sends you her regards,' said Lottie. 'She's looking forward to dining with you this evening.'

He grinned widely.

'Signor Moretti cannot talk before a performance,' explained the uniformed man.

The opera singer acknowledged him with a nod and grinned again. Lottie wondered if he had maintained his silence with Madame Lapointe.

'Mrs Moore says break a leg,' she added.

'Non.' The uniformed man wagged a finger at her. 'We say 'In bocca al lupo'.'

'Sorry. That then.'

'Crepi!' responded Signor Moretti.

'Oh. So you're allowed to say that then?'

Signor Moretti chuckled, then returned to his seat, a sign that it was time for her to leave.

LOTTIE JOINED Mrs Moore on the red velvet seats in the auditorium. She was staring through her opera glasses. 'I can't see a thing through these.' She placed her lorgnette in front of them. 'That's a little better. Or should it be the other way round?' She switched them and looked again. 'No, that's no better.'

'Any sign of Prince Manfred yet?'

'Not yet. But perhaps there will be once I've got these working properly. Have a look yourself and try to find him.'

'I don't know what he looks like.'

'Haven't you seen his portrait?'

'No.'

'He's handsome and has a fine nose.'

Lottie looked around for someone with these vague characteristics, but she was more captivated by the twinkling lights of the auditorium and how they illuminated the intricate gold moulding on every available surface. The effect was dazzling.

The orchestra began tuning up. 'What a racket,' joked Mrs Moore. 'I hope they get better than this.' Before long, the heavy curtain lifted, and the show began.

Amadeo Moretti strutted proudly on the stage with a cape and a three-cornered hat added to his costume. It was soon apparent to Lottie that Don Giovanni was a philanderer and Signor Moretti appeared to enjoy his role enormously. Although she appreciated the music, she grew weary of Don Giovanni's attempts to seduce the ladies on the stage. Picking up her opera glasses, she glanced around at the audience watching the show. Her attention was drawn to the boxes high up on either side of the stage. Surely Prince Manfred was sitting in one of them? But if he was, then how had he escaped Mrs Moore's notice?

It was then that she saw a pair of opera glasses pointed directly at her. Startled, she lowered hers and looked away. The man who held them was sitting in one of the boxes she had been watching and his gaze remained trained on her. She gave him a sidelong glance, trying to look at him without him noticing. He was a plump man with oiled black hair and aged about thirty. And still his gaze was directed straight at her.

Lottie felt her face heat up. Why wouldn't he look away?

Chapter Five

THE RESTAURANT of the Grand Hotel Splendore was lavish, yet comfortable. Every table was candlelit and the warm, cosy hue reflected in the shiny gold wallpaper and gilt-framed mirrors. Lottie tucked into a seafood risotto, enjoying its rich, creamy flavour.

'What a wonderful, absorbing performance you gave in Don Giovanni, Signor Moretti,' said Mrs Moore. 'I was quite overcome with emotion. Especially at the end, when you were dragged off to hell.'

'Thank you Mrs Moore, I'm most honoured that you enjoyed it.' He paused between mouthfuls to give a reverent nod. He'd changed into evening wear but kept his stage makeup on, perhaps hoping it improved his appearance. Lottie thought it fortunate he'd tucked his napkin into his collar because he'd splashed it with regular glugs of red wine.

'It's glorious to be in Venice again,' he said. 'Even though I'm from the south, I love Venice. I have no care for the north of Italy. Not even Milan. But Venice! It's my favourite. Have you been to Piazza San Marco yet?'

'Not yet,' said Mrs Moore. 'We only arrived today.'

'Ah! You must visit the Basilica di San Marco and see the relics of Saint Mark.' He chuckled. 'Let me tell you why I love the Venetians. You realise they stole the body of Saint Mark from Egypt?'

'No!'

'Oh yes. They built this beautiful city and decided something was missing. What was missing? Their very own saint! And so two merchants went to Alexandria and persuaded the priest at the church where Saint Mark lay that they should take him. They put Saint Mark's body in a wicker basket, carried it onto a boat and made the long, perilous journey up to Venice.'

'In a wicker basket? Good golly. When did this happen?'

'A thousand years ago. The relics have lain in the Basilica di San Marco ever since.'

'What a story!'

'I have many more stories of Venice if you'd like to hear them.'

'Oh, I would!'

The opera singer took a gulp of wine. 'I can't help noticing, Mrs Moore, that you're American.'

'That's right, although I claim Scottish ancestry.'

'Scottish?'

'My father was born in a shepherd's bothy in the Scottish Highlands,' said Mrs Moore.

'Bothy?'

'It's a type of hut. He emigrated to America as a boy and became a railroad tycoon.'

Amadeo Moretti grinned. 'A tycoon? He knew how to make money!'

'He certainly did.'

'And where's Mr Moore?'

'He left me.'

'No!'

'Yes. He ran off with a dancer from Petoskey.'

'Peto... what?'

'It's a small town in Michigan. On the lake, in fact. So we're divorced now.'

'Because it's on a lake?'

'No!' She gave a shriek of laughter. 'Oh, you are funny, Signor Moretti. My husband and I divorced because he ran off with the dancer.'

'I am sorry to hear it.'

'Oh, I was quite happy about it. He was my least favourite husband.'

'There was another one?'

'Two. My first husband died of rheumatic fever and my second husband died of drink.'

Signor Moretti glanced at the glass of wine in his hand and lowered it. 'Perhaps it will be fourth time lucky then, Mrs Moore?'

'Oh yes, I hope so. I'm after a title.'

'What sort of title?'

'My sister married an English lord, so if I can do better than that, my life will feel complete.'

'An English lord?' Signor Moretti regarded Mrs Moore with greater interest.

'Yes, Lord Buckley-Phipps. He comes from an ancient, aristocratic family which was very poor when he fell in love with my sister. An ancestor had gambled away most of their fortune. The family seat, Fortescue Manor, was practically crumbling into the ground. My sister rescued the house and the entire family with our father's money. You should see what she's done with Fortescue Manor, it's a magical place.'

'I should like to visit one day,' said Signor Moretti. 'Do you think she will allow it?'

'Of course she would! She adores entertaining. And any friend of mine is a friend of hers.'

'Wonderful! Let's drink to that! Although not too much because we don't want to die of it, do we?' He took another gulp from his glass.

The hotel manager, a tall man with a wide moustache, approached. 'I trust all is well with your meal this evening?'

'Oh, absolutely Signor Borelli!' shrilled Mrs Moore. 'And the company is enchanting.' She gestured at her companion.

'You are too kind,' chuckled Signor Moretti. They engaged in small talk with the manager for a few minutes before he went on his way to the next table. The singer turned back to Mrs Moore. 'So you are on the search for a husband. And, meanwhile, I am on the search for a wife.'

'Are you?'

'Oh yes. Perhaps the two of us could... you know...' He gave a wink.

'Oh, Signor Moretti! You're not Don Giovanni now, you know!' Mrs Moore's face turned the colour of a tomato and the pair dissolved into laughter.

Lottie felt her toes curl.

'Now what of Signorina Lottie here?' said the opera singer once they'd recovered themselves.

'I'm not looking for a husband,' said Lottie.

'Quite right, too. Are you descended from a tycoon or born in a shepherd's... what is it? Bothy?'

'My sister rescued her from an orphanage,' said Mrs Moore.

'Not rescued,' corrected Lottie. 'She hired me as a maid when I was fourteen. I was too old for the orphanage by then.'

'A little orphan,' beamed Signor Moretti. 'Like Rosina in the Barber of Seville!'

'Is that an opera?' asked Mrs Moore.

'Of course!'

'Do you live your life like an opera, Signor Moretti?'

'Of course!' They laughed again, and the singer drained

his glass before turning back to Lottie. 'Now let's not forget the reason that we're here this evening. It is to express my extreme gratitude to Signorina here. She reunited me with my beautiful Rosetta!' He pointed to the corgi who lay by his chair. Lottie looked down at her, and she returned the glance with her large brown eyes. 'If it wasn't for young Miss Sprigg, I would never have seen my beautiful dog again!'

'Oh surely you would have found her?' asked Mrs Moore.

'No I wouldn't, she would have fallen prey to the dog snatcher.'

'The dog snatcher? How awful!'

'It is terrible. I am told four dogs have been snatched in the past two weeks.'

'Who's taking them?' asked Mrs Moore.

'If we knew that, then they would have been locked up by now, wouldn't they? All we can do is keep a close eye on our beloved pets. Do you have any pets, Mrs Moore?'

'Oh no, animals make me sneeze.'

A wiry, grey-haired lady in a pink dress approached their table and greeted them in Italian. The smile fell from Mrs Moore's face as the visitor began an animated conversation with Signor Moretti. The lady looked about seventy, her hair was tied in a bun at the nape of her neck and she had keen, intelligent eyes.

Lottie finished her risotto and sat back to take in a display of ancient looking weapons on the wall. By the look of them, they'd probably been used in the barbaric medieval times. There was a long, curved sword and a couple of nasty-looking little daggers.

'Well, don't mind us,' said Mrs Moore after enduring the flow of Italian for a minute or so.

'Oh, I'm sorry.' The visitor turned to her. 'It was quite rude of me to interrupt. I couldn't resist saying hello to Signor

Moretti, such a talented baritone! My name is Mrs Harris, but please call me Jane. You sound like a fellow American to me.'

'I am. Mrs Moore.'

'Delighted to meet you.'

'This is my assistant, Miss Lottie Sprigg.'

'Hello!' said Lottie cheerily. She liked the look of the elderly lady with her kindly eyes and ability to speak fluent Italian.

'How long are you staying in Venice for?' Mrs Moore asked her.

'A week. I arrived yesterday, I've just completed a little tour of the Mediterranean. St Tropez, Corsica, Naples... and now here! I'm planning on visiting the eastern Mediterranean next, you can sail from here to Athens and Istanbul. I hope we get to stop off at Crete, too.'

'What a woman!' exclaimed the opera singer with an appreciative clap.

'Why, thank you! It's quite a lot for a little old lady from Wisconsin, I suppose.'

Signor Moretti pulled a chair from a neighbouring table. 'Please join us, Mrs Harris!'

'Oh, I don't want to interrupt.'

'I insist!'

'All right then.' She sat down. 'Where do you hail from, Mrs Moore?'

'Pennsylvania. My father was a railroad tycoon.'

'Was he indeed? How wonderful to meet you. There are so many interesting people staying here.'

'That's because we're staying at the Grand Hotel Splendore,' said Mrs Moore. 'One of the finest hotels in Venice.'

A waiter refilled their drinks, then Signor Moretti pulled off his napkin and got to his feet. 'Please excuse me, but I have just noticed an acquaintance of mine at the bar. I hope you don't think me rude, Mrs Moore, Mrs Harris, Miss Sprigg. I need to speak with him.' He gave a bow. 'It was wonderful to dine with you this evening.'

'And also with you,' said Mrs Moore. 'Perhaps we can do the same again tomorrow?'

'Oh, I'd like that,' said Mrs Harris.

'Tomorrow... I don't think I'll be able to make it tomorrow,' he replied. 'But as we are staying in the same hotel, I am quite sure I shall see you all around.'

They watched as the opera singer strode over to the bar, his dog at his heels, and joined a grey-haired gentleman in tweed.

'Colonel Pickering,' said Mrs Harris.

'Colonel Pickering?' Mrs Moore picked up her lorgnette and observed the pair. 'Who's he?'

'Mrs Moore! Am I right?' Lottie startled at the impeccable English accent which came from a young, plump man with oiled hair. 'Sorry! I didn't mean to make you all jump. May I?' He gestured at the seat which the opera singer had just vacated.

'Erm, yes,' said Mrs Moore. 'How do you know my name?'

'We've met before! Perhaps I'm not particularly memorable.' He chuckled. 'It was at a party at Fortescue Manor.'

Lottie recognised him as the man who'd been staring at her through his opera glasses. There'd been nothing creepy about him after all, he'd merely recognised her employer.

'Fortescue Manor?' said Mrs Moore. 'That's my sister's place!'

'No! Really?'

'Yes!'

'How nice to meet you Mr...'

'Cecil-Raikes,' he replied. 'William Cecil-Raikes.' He wore a striped evening suit and a yellow velvet bow tie.

'Please don't think me rude,' said Mrs Moore. 'But I don't recall you or your name. Where are your family from?'

'South west England.'

'How lovely, I've never been there. Is it beautiful?'

'Exquisite. I spotted you at the opera earlier and now it's a coincidence to find you here too.'

'Well, it's delightful to make your acquaintance again, Mr Cecil-Raikes,' Mrs Moore said.

'William, please. In fact, call me Billy! No need for formality, particularly as we're all enjoying ourselves here in beautiful Venice.' He struck Lottie as the carefree, jolly type with chubby, boyish cheeks reddened with exuberance.

Mrs Moore introduced Mrs Harris and Lottie. 'And what brings you to Venice, Billy?' she asked.

'I'm doing the Grand Tour! It's a little old-fashioned now, I realise that. But I'm following in the footsteps of those chaps who paved the way in the olden days.'

'Good for you!' said Mrs Harris. 'Where've you been so far?'

'Paris, then Geneva, Turin, Padua and Bologna. After Venice I'm off to Rome, then Naples, Sicily and onto Malta. I shall journey back via Germany, probably stop off at Berlin, and then head over to Amsterdam before returning to old Blighty.'

'I'm exhausted just hearing about it,' said Mrs Moore.

'Me too,' said Mrs Harris. 'And I thought my tour of the Mediterranean was tiring.'

'You're touring the Mediterranean?' said Billy. 'You must tell me all about it. But first, I'll order us some champagne. Then we can raise a toast to new friends!'

LOTTIE TOOK in the evening air on Mrs Moore's balcony when they returned to the room after dinner. Twinkling lights reflected in the Grand Canal and the sky was a starry indigo dome. The flowers unleashed a heady, floral scent after basking in the sunshine all day. Lottie had never visited a place like this before, it was a far cry from the draughty orphanage.

She peeked at the surrounding balconies, wondering if anyone else was out here, too. Some were in darkness, whereas others were cast in a muted golden light from a bedroom lamp. She couldn't see anyone else about. From somewhere nearby, a bell struck midnight.

'Can you come back inside and close the shutters, Lottie?' came Mrs Moore's voice from the room. 'I don't want mosquitoes getting in.'

Lottie sighed, she wanted to spend a little longer out here. Her box room didn't have a balcony, she had to make do with peering out of the window instead. She turned to go inside, then paused when she heard a shout.

It was a man's voice, but there was still no sign of anyone else. All she could hear now was the water lapping at the foot of the building. Had she imagined the shout? There had been anger in the voice. A disagreement perhaps. Possibly influenced by drink.

The shout came again, and then some words mumbled after it. Was it above or below her? To one side? It felt disorientating. There was little doubt it had come from one of the rooms, though.

'Lottie!'

'Coming!' She stepped inside and closed the doors and shutters.

Chapter Six

LOTTIE WOKE AT SEVEN, washed at the little hand basin in her room and put on her blue, cotton day dress. Mrs Moore was a late riser, so she had some time to herself. Venice called to her from beyond the window of her box room and she itched to get outside for an early morning walk. She wanted to see the streets before they grew busy with tourists. She pulled a comb through her hair, put on her walking shoes and crept out via the little hallway as Mrs Moore's snores rumbled from beyond her closed door.

In the shiny marble hotel lobby, a handful of staff were huddled in a group, talking in hushed tones. *Perhaps they're discussing tasks for the day ahead*, Lottie thought as she headed for the doors. Two police officers in blue uniform passed her and more police officers were gathered outside in the square. Lottie now sensed something out of the ordinary was happening. Although she wanted to go for a walk, she was also keen to find out what was going on. She paused for a moment, wondering what to do.

'Psst!' came a noise from behind her. She turned to see the

red-uniformed bellboy beckoning to her from an alleyway at the side of the hotel.

'Has something happened?' she asked as she approached him.

'You haven't heard?' he replied. 'Where have you been?' He put a thin, little cigarette to his lips and inhaled.

'I was asleep. You do realise it's only a quarter-past seven?'

'There's been a murder.'

Lottie gasped. 'Here?'

The bellboy nodded. 'He was found in the Grand Canal with a knife in his back.'

'*What*?'

'He must have been stabbed, then pushed off his balcony.'

'When?'

'Last night.'

'Have they caught the person who did it?'

'Not yet.'

Lottie shuddered. 'So the murderer is still on the loose?'

'I think so.'

'In the hotel?'

He shrugged. 'I don't know.'

'How horrible! Who was murdered?'

'He was an opera singer. Amadeo Moretti.'

'Signor Moretti?' said Mrs Moore as Lottie related the news to her. She sat propped up against her pillows, bed jacket over her shoulders and coffee cup in hand. 'Who could possibly murder Amadeo Moretti? We only dined with him last night. There was no sign he was going to get murdered, was there?'

'No. But I don't suppose there would be.'

'When did it happen?'

'Last night, but I don't know the time. All I know is what the bellboy told me.'

'You'll have to speak to him again and get more information.'

'I don't think he has any more information.'

'But he will do. He works here, he'll hear about everything that's going on.'

'I'll ask him if I see him.' Lottie gave a shiver. 'Perhaps we should move to another hotel?'

'Move? Absolutely not, I won't hear of it. This hotel is where everything is happening and we're at the very centre of it. Once I've had my breakfast, I shall get started on my correspondence. Everyone at home will be clamouring to hear about this.'

Breakfast in the restaurant was a subdued affair, with guests and staff talking in hushed tones. Mrs Moore wore black satin and Lottie privately marvelled that she'd had the foresight to pack a mourning dress.

Billy approached their table. He wore a black suit with a black bow tie and his oiled hair was combed back from his dour, plump face. 'Do you mind if I join you?' he asked. 'I can't bear the thought of eating alone, I need someone to talk to.'

'You're more than welcome, Billy,' replied Mrs Moore. 'Lottie here has found out some of the detail. Have you heard much?'

'No. All I know is that a great opera singer is now dead, and I didn't get a chance to say more than a few words to him.' He pulled a handkerchief from his jacket pocket and mopped his brow. 'I never thought anything as awful as this would happen in a beautiful city like Venice.'

'Neither did I,' replied Mrs Moore. 'It's almost ruined Venice for me.'

Lottie listened as she quietly ate her boiled egg. Just a short distance from her was the table they'd sat at the previous evening. She gazed sadly at the chair which Signor Moretti had occupied, then looked at the bar where he'd joined Colonel Pickering.

Who was Colonel Pickering? And what did he make of Signor Moretti's death?

As Lottie glanced around, she noticed something different about the wall.

'What are you staring at, Lottie?' asked Mrs Moore.

'The weapons, those medieval style ones. They were displayed on the wall over there, but they've been taken away.'

'I don't remember those.'

'Lottie's right,' said Billy. 'I saw them too. They were quite fearsome, as I recall. I suppose they were on display because they were extremely old and interesting, but I remember thinking that somebody could do a terrible mischief with them. Oh dear, I don't suppose...?'

Lottie spotted the bellboy passing through the room. 'I'll go and find out,' she said, taking her napkin from her lap and placing it next to her plate.

She caught up with the bellboy in the lobby. 'Excuse me,' she said. 'So sorry to interrupt. I'm Lottie, by the way. I should have introduced myself sooner.'

He smiled. 'I'm Stefano. I'm sorry I had to give you such sad news first thing this morning. Are you alright?'

'I think so. How about you? It must be very upsetting for you and your colleagues.'

'It is. We've had plenty of customers die in the hotel before, but we've never had a murder. Everybody's very shocked.'

'I was wondering, do you know why the old weapons have been taken off the wall?'

Stefano gave a slow nod. 'One of them was used in the murder.'

'No!'

'I'm afraid so. They've been locked in the safe now.'

'Which one?' Lottie could recall the sharp blades and winced as she did so.

'The cinquedea.'

'The what?'

'It's a type of dagger, very old. From the sixteenth century. It was the smallest knife on the wall, so I suppose the murderer could have hidden it in his clothing. His room was on the same corridor as yours.'

Lottie felt her skin prickle. 'Amadeo Moretti's room?'

'Yes, room twenty-two. You're twenty-five, aren't you?'

'Yes.'

'But don't worry, I'm sure the murderer was only after him.'

'Why do you say that?'

'He didn't attack anyone else last night and he could have done. There must have been something about Signor Moretti.'

His attention turned to a dark-suited gentleman who was now striding across the lobby. He had a creased, careworn expression and a quiff of greying hair. A group of police officers followed behind him. 'Here comes Commissario Romeo,' said Stefano. 'He'll find the murderer, no problem.'

'Romeo?'

'He doesn't like jokes about his name.'

'Who said I was going to joke about it?'

They exchanged smiles.

'Stefano!' Signor Borelli's head appeared from behind a door.

'I have to go.' The bellboy went on his way.

Chapter Seven

'AFTER LAST NIGHT'S awful incident, it seems disrespectful to enjoy ourselves sightseeing,' said Mrs Moore. 'I think it would be better to sit quietly in the lounge. I can catch up on my correspondence there.' Lottie suspected her employer wished to hang around at the hotel so she could keep a close eye on proceedings.

The lounge overlooked the Grand Canal which appealed less to Lottie now that she knew Amadeo Moretti had been found floating in it. The upper portion of the tall windows was draped with elaborate satin curtains which reminded Lottie of ladies' petticoats. Mrs Moore arranged herself on a gold velvet chair in the corner of the lounge and assumed a mournful expression. She set out her letter writing parapher-nalia next to a bowl of fruit on the low table in front of her, then picked up her lorgnette and observed the comings and goings.

Lottie brought a scruffy paperback of detective stories with her and a notebook in which she intended to document her travels. The notebook was empty and, given the tragic event, it was difficult to imagine writing anything in it soon.

It was also difficult finding the concentration to read. Hushed conversations around her piqued Lottie's interest. Who knew what? And who were they telling about it? She could only read a few lines at a time before glancing up again and trying to glean what was going on.

About a quarter of an hour had passed when the commissario strode in with a young, bespectacled man in tow. His heavy brow was knotted into a frown and he inhaled on a cigarette. To Lottie's surprise, he headed directly for them.

'Mrs Moore? I'm Commissario Romeo and this is my deputy.' He gestured at the bespectacled man. 'I would like a word with you, please.'

'Me?' Her mouth hung open.

'Yes.'

'Why?'

'I can explain.' He pulled a chair up to the table with the bowl of fruit on it. The deputy lingered behind him.

'Romeo, did you say?'

'Yes. A relatively common name here in Italy so you can forget about any Shakespeare jokes.'

'I can see you're in no mood for jokes, Commissario.'

'Exactly.' He opened his notebook, took out a small slip of paper, and held it up for Mrs Moore to look at. 'Do you recognise this?'

Mrs Moore squinted at it. 'No, I don't.'

He showed it to Lottie. 'Do you, Signorina?'

Lottie examined the few words written on it: "Sorry you fell into the canal."

'I haven't seen it before,' she said.

'Are you sure about that?'

'Quite sure.'

'Why would we recognise it, Commissario?' asked Mrs Moore.

'It was a note you gave to Signor Moretti.'

'I didn't. That's not my handwriting. Nor Lottie's for that matter. So I'm afraid you're mistaken, Commissario.'

'This young lady,' he pointed at Lottie, 'visited Signor Moretti in his dressing room and gave him a bouquet of roses before his performance yesterday evening. The note was found in the flowers.'

'But we didn't write it!'

'The note predicts his fate, don't you think? He was found in the canal and this message says, "Sorry you fell into the canal."'

'I know what's happened here,' said Mrs Moore. 'Someone else wrote that note and we never saw it. The roses were given to me by a gondolier after I fell off his gondola into the canal. The flowers and the note were an apology.'

'That's right,' said Lottie, keen to emphasise their innocence.

The commissario glowered at them then made some notes. 'What's the gondolier's name?' he asked.

'I don't know,' said Mrs Moore. 'It's not on the note, is it?'

'Strange, don't you think?'

'A little, I suppose.' She cast a nervous glance at Lottie.

'Why did you give Signor Moretti the flowers?' he asked.

'They were to thank him for inviting us to Don Giovanni.'

'But these flowers were also a gift to you?'

'Yes.'

'Why did you give away your gift?'

'The invitation to the opera was made at the last moment and we didn't have time to arrange another gift for him.'

The commissario inhaled on his cigarette then addressed Lottie. 'What did you speak to Signor Moretti about, Miss Sprigg?'

'Nothing.'

'Nothing?'

'He couldn't speak because he was resting his voice for the evening's performance.'

'So to be clear, Miss Sprigg. You took the flowers to Signor Moretti, but he said nothing?'

'He said "crepi" after I wished him luck. But that was all he said.'

'I see.' He made some more notes.

'Are you interviewing everyone who visited him in his dressing room before the performance?' Lottie asked.

He nodded. 'We need to speak to everyone who had dealings with him yesterday.'

'Have you spoken to Madame Lapointe?'

'No. Who's she?'

'She's staying at this hotel and I saw her coming out of Signor Moretti's dressing room just before I went in.'

'Did you?' asked Mrs Moore. 'You didn't tell me that!'

'I forgot.'

The commissario made a note. 'Madame Lapointe,' he muttered.

'Camille Lapointe,' explained Mrs Moore. 'French. A writer. She's in room fourteen.'

The detective turned to his deputy and issued an instruction. Then he addressed Mrs Moore again. 'While I'm here, is there anything else you'd like to tell me?'

'We dined with Signor Moretti last night,' said Mrs Moore.

'And how did he appear to you?'

'Very well.'

'Did he seem bothered by anything?'

'If he was, he certainly didn't show it. And then he went off to speak to Colonel Pickering.'

'Yes, I'm aware of that.'

'You've spoken to the colonel?'

'In great detail.'

'Then I think that's probably all we can help you with.'

'Very well.' He folded up his notebook.

Lottie wondered what the colonel knew. 'Was Colonel Pickering the last person to see Signor Moretti alive?' she asked.

'We believe so,' said the commissario. 'Unless there was someone else who isn't admitting to it.'

'What time was the murder?'

'The doctor thinks it was between midnight and one o'clock.'

'I think I heard something!'

'You did?'

She told him about the angry shout she'd heard just after midnight as she stood on the balcony. 'Perhaps I overheard an argument between Signor Moretti and someone else?' she said.

'You may have done.' He reopened his notebook and made more notes. 'Did you hear what was said?'

'No, I didn't.'

'I shall probably need to speak to you about that again, Miss Sprigg. And you will both do yourselves a favour by remembering the name of the gondolier. Until I can find him and verify your story, I'm afraid I remain rather suspicious about the note in the flowers.'

'How ridiculous!' said Mrs Moore once the commissario and his deputy had left. 'How could he possibly think we wrote that note? If we were planning to murder Signor Moretti and push him into the canal, then we were hardly going to warn him about it in a note, were we? And to think that Romeo is the most senior police officer in Venice!'

'Is he?'

'He must be. I'm afraid to say that, with him in charge, they've probably got little hope of finding the murderer. You really must check bunches of flowers for notes in future, Lottie. Missing that one is causing us an awful lot of bother. I wish we could find that gondolier again. You need to go out and find him.'

'But he could be anywhere! There must be hundreds of gondoliers in Venice.'

'I realise that. But without him confirming that he wrote that note, we risk being in trouble. Perhaps you can have a look for him while I write my letters.'

'Now?'

'Yes. Oh what a mess. I'm beginning to wish we'd never met Signor Moretti now!'

LOTTIE STEPPED out of the hotel and made her way down the alleyway at its side to the quiet little canal Mrs Moore had fallen in. About a hundred yards to her right, the canal joined with the Grand Canal. A police boat was moored outside the hotel's water door. There was no path alongside that section of the canal, so she couldn't walk that way. There was a path on her left, so she took that route, convinced she would never see the gondolier again. How many miles of canal were there in Venice? It was the sort of fact she could find in a book easily enough.

A man stood on the path up ahead, looking at something in his hand. He was dressed in tweed and wore a boater hat. His stooped gait suggested he was an older gentleman, and he seemed familiar.

Catching sight of Lottie, he pushed something into his pocket but appeared to misjudge it. 'Bother!' he cried as a wad of bank notes scattered onto the ground. A breeze whisked some towards Lottie and she managed to stop all but one from being blown into the canal. She hurriedly gathered up the salmon pink notes and saw each one was worth five hundred lire.

'Here you are,' she handed the elderly gentleman the notes to add to his pile. 'There's one in the canal I'm afraid.' She pointed at it floating gently away to the Grand Canal.

'Bless you, what a kind young lady you are.' He smiled. His complexion was lined and freckled, as if he'd spent years in sunny climes. The prominent feature on his face was a grey moustache, waxed into a fine point at each end. 'Very kind indeed. You could have easily run off with those, couldn't you? And bought yourself a nice new dress or whatever young ladies spend their money on these days. Shoes perhaps.'

'Colonel Pickering, isn't it? I recognise you from the hotel.'

'Why, yes I am.'

'I'm Miss Sprigg, Lottie Sprigg. I'm staying at the hotel with my employer, Mrs Moore.'

'The American heiress? I've heard about her.'

He thumbed through the notes in his hand and Lottie estimated there were fifty there. Possibly sixty. He folded the pile and pushed it into his jacket pocket. A possible thirty thousand lire. Lottie did some quick sums in her head and worked out it would take her a year to earn that amount of money.

'There's erm... probably no need to mention this to anybody,' he said with a smile. He patted his pocket. 'People can get a bit funny about money, you know how it is.'

'Of course.'

'Amadeo Moretti told me about Mrs Moore last night. You dined with him, I believe? I should like to meet her...' He gazed down at the canal and sighed. 'Dreadful business. Someone murdered the chap. Unfathomable.'

'Did you know him well?' Lottie asked.

'No, not well. Awful shock. I'd better get to the bank now. Nice meeting you, Miss Sprigg. I'll leave you to walk on ahead of me, your legs are faster than mine. Arrivederci, as they say here!'

Lottie bid him farewell and walked on ahead, wondering if she should be suspicious about the colonel's money or not.

AFTER A FRUITLESS HOUR-LONG search for the gondolier, Lottie returned to the hotel. There was no sign of Mrs Moore in the lounge, so she made her way to the room. She climbed the staircase, walked along the corridor, and noticed a tapping noise on the marble behind her. She turned to see Signor Moretti's corgi.

'Oh, Rosetta! You poor little thing!' The dog sat as Lottie made an affectionate fuss of her. 'Who's been looking after you? Oh dear... I suppose no one's been looking after you, have they? They're too busy working out what happened to your owner. Oh no, you're orphaned!' She knelt down and gave the dog a hug. 'Just like me.'

She released Rosetta who calmly regarded her with large brown eyes. 'I don't suppose you've had any breakfast yet, have you? I think I can find someone who can help.'

Lottie made her way back downstairs, and the dog followed. After searching the lobby and the lounge, she found Stefano walking out of the restaurant with a large box. 'This is Signor Moretti's dog,' she said.

'I remember seeing him with it now.'

'Her, it's a *she*. Rosetta.'

'Who's looking after her?' he asked.

'No one I suppose. She needs food, are there any leftovers in the kitchen?'

'I'll have a look.'

She followed Stefano to the kitchen door. He placed his

box on the floor, went inside and reappeared with some offcuts of meat, bread crusts and some dried-up scrambled egg.

'Perfect!' said Lottie. Rosetta consumed it all within five seconds.

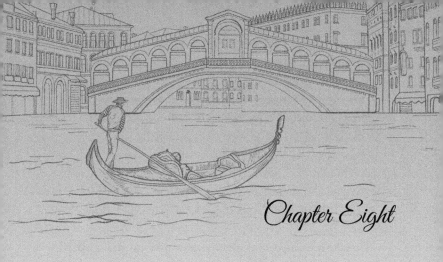

Chapter Eight

Colonel Pickering lost his way a few times. 'Every street looks the same,' he muttered to himself. He eventually found the bank in a dingy corner of a square. The heavy door had ornate hinges which curled across the woodwork like cast iron ivy. A little bell sat above a tiny brass plaque announcing the name of the institution.

The colonel pressed the bell and hummed to himself as he waited. It was unfortunate he'd dropped his money and even more unfortunate that someone had seen him do it. The English girl seemed pleasant enough, but could she be trusted?

A pale-faced bank clerk in a dark suit admitted him. Colonel Pickering stepped over to a substantial desk and sank into a leather chair. The clerk took a seat opposite him.

Little daylight entered via the small, barred windows. Instead, the room was lit by a handful of orange-hued table lamps. A grandfather clock ticked noisily.

'Another deposit,' said the colonel, pulling the wad of notes from his pocket and plonking it onto the leather-topped desk. 'Nearly lost it in the canal on my way here! It was a close shave, I can tell you.'

The clerk gave the colonel a thin, yet polite smile and counted out the notes. Another gentleman emerged from a side door and placed a small cup of espresso in front of the colonel. 'Darned decent of you, young chap,' he said.

Once the clerk had finished counting, he dipped an elegant fountain pen into an inkpot, inscribed a number onto a slip of paper, and presented it to the colonel.

'Looks about right,' said the colonel. He drank down his espresso.

The clerk nodded, unlocked a drawer in his desk, placed the money inside, locked it again, then wrote out an immaculate remittance slip. He took care over his lettering and the pen nib scratched audibly on the thick paper. He blotted it with another piece of paper, then presented it to the colonel. Colonel Pickering took it, folded it, and placed it in the inside pocket of his jacket. 'Pleasure doing business with you,' he said to the clerk, holding out his hand. The clerk shook it and gave another thin smile.

BACK OUT IN THE SQUARE, the colonel felt buoyed by the coffee and the safe deposit of the money. Then the recollection of Signor Moretti's death crept up on him.

'Dear oh dear,' he said, rubbing at his chin. 'A very great pity indeed.' The commissario had questioned him extensively that morning. Before breakfast! He'd warned the man he was no good in the mornings until he'd had a boiled egg and toast, but the Italian detective hadn't listened to him and insisted on firing questions at him. No manners at all! No one would have tried such a thing back in his army days. But that was when he had authority and respect. How soon those things vanished after retirement.

He'd done all he could to cover himself. All he could do

now was hope the young Englishwoman didn't tell anyone about the money.

Chapter Nine

AFTER A LONG AND TORTUROUS DISCUSSION, Mrs Moore agreed Lottie could keep Rosetta until the end of the day. It wasn't the perfect solution, but Lottie reasoned it was better than nothing. 'You'll need to find someone else to take her on,' added Mrs Moore. 'We can't possibly have her with us, not when we're travelling. It simply isn't practical.' She then requested some peace for a rest, as she had another headache coming on.

Lottie returned to the lounge with her book and took Rosetta with her. The pair made themselves comfortable in the corner. Three police officers sat at a table close by but swiftly got to their feet when Commissario Romeo put in an appearance. He barked a command at them and they followed him out of the room, adjusting their hats as they went.

The hotel manager, Signor Borelli, strode into the room with Stefano the bellboy in tow. He pointed at a marble statue of a scantily clad nymph, then pointed to the other end of the room. Once the manager had left, Stefano spotted Lottie.

'Are you going to be Rosetta's new owner?' he asked, looking at the dozing dog.

'Only until the end of today. I have to find someone else to look after her, but I don't know who.'

'Surely your employer won't allow her to be left out on the street with the dog snatcher about?'

'I hope not, but I wouldn't bet on it.'

Stefano lowered his voice. 'Apparently, the masked man was seen near this hotel last night.'

Lottie felt a chill in her stomach. 'The masked man? Who's he?'

'Some people think he's the dog snatcher, but now they're saying he's the murderer!'

'Really? What does he look like?'

'He wears a mask and a cloak.'

'Why?'

'To hide his identity, of course. He could be anyone, couldn't he? He wears a plague doctor mask.'

'What's that?'

'The mask of il medico della peste. It has a long, curved nose which looks like a beak. He wears a hood, so all you see is his white mask and two dark holes where his eyes stare out at you.'

Lottie shivered. 'He sounds terrifying!'

'One of the waiters saw him on an evening walk a few weeks ago. He was so frightened, he ran back to his room and wouldn't come out for two days. Signor Borelli was furious.'

'And what did the masked man do?'

'Nothing. He just stood and stared at him. The waiter said it was worse than being attacked.'

'Perhaps it's just someone playing a joke?'

'It might be, but it's not a very funny joke, is it?'

'Maybe if he were confronted, he would turn out not to be quite so scary after all.'

'I don't think so. Everybody here thinks he's likely to have been the murderer.'

'But if he was the murderer, then why draw attention to himself in a mask and cloak?'

'I don't know.'

'And why would he kill Amadeo Moretti?'

'I don't know that either.'

'I've thought of another suspect,' she whispered.

Stefano leaned in to hear. 'Who?'

'Colonel Pickering. Commissario Romeo told us he was the last person to see the opera singer alive. I saw the colonel this morning, and he dropped a large amount of money. I helped him pick it up. Perhaps the money has something to do with Signor Moretti's murder, or perhaps it has nothing to do with it. But it was rather odd.'

'I wonder why he was carrying lots of money about?'

'And I'll tell you something else suspicious too,' said Lottie, 'I saw the French lady, Madame Lapointe, coming out of Signor Moretti's dressing room just before the show last night. I'm sure she saw me, but she hurried away as if she didn't want to be noticed.'

'That sounds suspicious, but maybe she had a simple explanation for visiting him.'

'Perhaps. But when I told her I was going to the opera, she neither told me she was going nor that she knew Signor Moretti. Why would she hide that information?'

'Maybe she's just a private person?'

'Maybe she is.'

'It sounds quite complicated and the police are already busy.'

'With what?'

'There was a robbery at the archaeological museum last week. There's the dog snatcher to catch and also the jewel thief, too.'

'Jewel thief?'

'My father works in a jeweller's shop on the Ponte Rialto. It's a bridge. Have you seen it yet? It's a very famous bridge.'

'Not yet.'

'According to my father, there were some jewellery thefts in Milan a few weeks ago. A lady stole diamonds using clever sleight of hand. The Milan police questioned someone she was acquainted with and the rumour is she's now in Venice. Commissario Romeo has a lot to do at the moment.'

Lottie glanced down at the corgi dozing by her feet. 'But Rosetta needs justice. She must be missing her owner terribly.'

'She must be.'

'They need to find Signor Moretti's murderer for her sake.'

'Stefano!' Signor Borelli had returned to the room and was pointing at the statue.

'Oops, I have to go.'

LOTTIE WATCHED Stefano move the statue across the room and wondered if there was something she could do about the murder investigation. She had once identified the culprit who'd been stealing chalk from the orphanage classroom. She'd only been eleven at the time, but her investigation had included surveillance and interviews before laying a trap for the thief. Although it hadn't been a serious crime, she'd been proud of her sleuthing skills.

A murder investigation was quite different, though, and there could be danger involved too.

Rosetta sat up and placed a paw on Lottie's knee.

'You're not hungry again, are you? It's not been long since your breakfast.'

Lottie wondered what Signor Moretti would usually have done with his dog at this time. Dogs liked routine, she recalled that from the many spaniels at Fortescue Hall.

'My guess is you'd like a walk,' she said.

LOTTIE AND ROSETTA stepped out into the sunny piazza where they'd first met. As they passed the cafe tables, Lottie caught sight of someone in a pink hat waving at her.

'Cooee!' It was Jane Harris, seated at one of the tables. 'Would you like to join me for an espresso?'

Lottie agreed and made herself comfortable on a cafe chair.

'I see you've got his dog.' Mrs Harris patted Rosetta's head. 'How nice of you to look after her.'

'It's only for today unfortunately. And I need to buy her a lead.'

'Surely Signor Moretti had one for her?'

'Yes, but I don't think it's a good time to be looking through his belongings for it.'

'Perhaps not right now. But get a cheap one for today and I'm sure you can get hold of her usual lead later.' Mrs Harris summoned a waiter and ordered two espressos. Lottie opened her purse. 'No, no, I won't hear of it.' Mrs Harris tapped her on the wrist. 'The espresso's on me. I think we could all do with a bit of extra coffee this morning, couldn't we? I can't believe Signor Moretti is dead. Who would want to do a thing like that? And in such a manner, too! Stabbed and thrown off his balcony into the canal.' She gave a shudder. 'Some people are barbaric. You know, we once had a similar thing happen in my hometown.'

'Really?'

'Yes, a famous singer was shot dead in his house late one night. Everyone thought it had just been an intruder, a robbery gone wrong. But it turned out he had an extremely complicated life. There was ill-gotten money, love affairs, secret children, revenge, misunderstandings, all that sort of thing. It was quite a job for the police to sort out, I can tell you. Everybody had a theory about what had happened, but I'm pleased to say that my theory was correct.'

'You found out who did it?'

'More or less. My nephew works in law enforcement and I had a word in his ear and they got the guy all right.'

'So, what did you do to work it out?'

'It's a long story. But if you've got a bit of time, I can tell you all about it.'

Chapter Ten

'WHAT BRINGS YOU TO VENICE, Madame Lapointe?' asked Commissario Romeo. The pair sat in the lounge and puffed clouds of tobacco smoke at each other.

They spoke in Italian. The commissario had attempted some broken French before Camille assured him she spoke his own language well. She picked an imaginary speck of dust from the lapel of her dark woollen dress, keen to project an air of nonchalance.

'I came here to heal a broken heart,' she said.

Her reply seemed to throw him off-balance, which had been her intention. If she could unsettle him, then hopefully he couldn't get all the information he wanted. His eyebrows gave a little dance before eventually settling again. 'How long do you plan to stay for?' he asked.

'For as long as it takes for my heart to heal.' She held his gaze, and he looked away to make some notes.

'Where are you from in France?' he asked.

'Biarritz.'

'Are you married?'

'Why do you want to know?'

'For background.'

'And what if I don't want to say?'

'It will look better if you cooperate, Madame Lapointe.'

She batted her eyelashes. 'Why don't you guess?'

He sighed and ran a hand across his brow. 'I don't have time for games, Madame Lapointe. I have to speak to many people today. Married? Yes or no?'

'No.'

'Thank you.' He made a note. 'Do you have any employment?'

'I'm a writer.'

'Are you? What do you write?'

'Love stories.' She emphasised the first word and noticed his eyebrows twitch again.

'My wife likes reading love stories,' he said.

'Then she's a lady of impeccable taste.' She followed this with a smile and noticed one corner of his mouth lift.

'How did you know Amadeo Moretti?' he asked.

'I didn't.' It was a lie, and she had to hope he believed it.

'No?'

'No.'

'Did you ever meet him?'

'I saw him here at the hotel and I knew who he was.'

'Did you speak to him?'

'No.' She lifted her chin and puffed a ring of smoke into the air.

'Where were you between the hours of eleven o'clock yesterday evening and one o'clock this morning?'

'I was in my room.'

'Can anyone confirm that?'

'Are you asking if I had company?'

He cleared his throat. 'Not necessarily. A member of the hotel staff could have called at your room, for example.'

'No one did. I was on my own. More's the pity.'

'And you're quite sure that you didn't know Signor Moretti? Or ever spoke to him?'

'Quite sure.'

He sat back in his chair and gave an exhale which vibrated his lips. 'That's interesting. Because a lady matching your description was seen visiting Signor Moretti in his dressing room shortly before last night's show.'

So the English girl has talked, thought Camille. She'd wondered if she might. She decided to feign ignorance. 'I visited him in his dressing room? Impossible.'

'Perhaps you can tell me where you were at half-past six yesterday evening?'

'In my room here. On my own. As usual.' She pushed out her lower lip in mock sadness.

'So you deny visiting Signor Moretti in his dressing room?'

'Absolutely. Whoever told you that must have been mistaken.'

'Very well.' He closed his notebook, and she wondered what he knew about her. Much more than he was letting on, she suspected. 'Thank you for your time, Madame Lapointe. I may need to speak to you again.'

'I look forward to it, Commissario.'

He got up from his chair. 'You speak excellent Italian, by the way, how did you learn it so well?'

'From my Italian lovers.' It was another lie, and she accompanied it with a wink to make him feel even more uncomfortable. She enjoyed watching his eyebrows twitch again, and he pulled at his collar as if it was too tight.

'Very well. Au revoir, Madame.'

'Au revoir.' Camille's smile faded as she watched the Commissario walk away with his deputy. Had she done enough? Perhaps he would doubt what the English girl had told him. But all he had to do was find another witness who'd seen her with Signor Moretti and she was in serious trouble.

Chapter Eleven

MRS MOORE WAS STILL LANGUISHING in bed when Lottie returned to the hotel room with Rosetta later that afternoon. The scent of rosewater pervaded the air, Mrs Moore liked to use it liberally when she was feeling under the weather.

'I bought a lead for Rosetta,' said Lottie. 'And I had a long conversation with Jane Harris.'

'I'm sure she could talk the hind leg off a donkey.'

'She was quite interesting, actually. She told me about a murder case she helped solve in her hometown in Wisconsin.'

'She helped solve a murder?' A knock at the door interrupted them. 'Oh no, if that's the police, then shoo them away, please Lottie. They can't possibly believe we murdered Signor Moretti because of some silly note they found in the flowers. Have you found that gondolier yet?'

'Not yet,' said Lottie, as she walked over to the door and opened it.

'Miss Sprigg! How wonderful to see a friendly face!'

Billy marched past her and sank into one of the fringed chairs by the table. 'Hello Mrs Moore,' he said, seemingly unbothered by the fact she was resting in bed. 'Feeling tired? Isn't it a dreadful day?'

'I've known better days.'

He took his handkerchief from his pocket and mopped his brow. 'I've had the police speaking to me. Have they spoken to you?'

'They have indeed,' said Mrs Moore. 'That Romeo chap.'

'That's the one. Rather crabby, isn't he? I can't imagine there being a Juliet where he's concerned.'

'Apparently he doesn't like jokes being made about his name,' said Mrs Moore.

'And I don't like being questioned as though I've done something wrong! He reminds me of one of my masters at Eton. I felt like I was being scolded in the schoolroom again.'

'Poor Billy,' said Mrs Moore.

'Yes, poor me. Do you have any tea?'

'I'm afraid not. Lottie, perhaps you can call for some?'

Lottie telephoned reception and asked for tea to be brought to the room.

'I haven't had a decent cup of tea since...' Billy shook his head. 'I don't know when. England probably! Much as I'm enjoying the grand tour, I can't wait to get back home again for a decent cuppa. It's just not the same anywhere else. No one outside Britain knows what to do with tea leaves. They either steep them for hours in lukewarm water or stew up a pot that has barely a tea leaf in it!'

'What did the police ask you, Mr Cecil-Raikes?' asked Lottie.

'Oh, call me Billy, just like Mrs Moore does. The usual questions. Did I know Signor Moretti? What was I doing when he died? All that sort of thing. I had absolutely nothing to tell them, of course. I saw him talking to Colonel Pickering at the bar when I had a drink with you, and that was all. I suppose they have to ask everyone the same questions, but they're very good at making you feel you've done something wrong when you haven't.'

'Who do you think murdered Signor Moretti?' asked Lottie.

'Golly, what a question!' He crossed his legs and thought. 'I haven't a clue. I suppose it could have been just about anyone, couldn't it? I only ever had a few words with him and I wish I'd got to know him better. He gave such a wonderful performance on his final night.'

'Lottie heard him arguing with someone just before the knife was plunged in,' said Mrs Moore.

'Did you?' Billy's eyes widened.

'I heard an argument,' clarified Lottie. 'But I can't be sure if it was Signor Moretti. It could have been someone else.'

'Where was the argument?'

'In one of the rooms which had its windows open last night. I was out on the balcony.'

'Oh, let's see!' He jumped up from his seat. 'Through here?' He opened the doors which led to the balcony and Lottie followed him.

He glanced around at the neighbouring balconies. 'Did you see him on one of these?'

'No, I didn't see him at all. And I can't be completely sure it was him, I just heard an argument.'

'I wonder which room was his?'

'Twenty-two, apparently. This is room twenty-five. Room twenty-two is that way.' She pointed to their right.

Billy counted the balconies. 'Just three balconies along from here! You could well have overheard it all.' He looked down at the canal. 'Quite a drop, isn't it? What would you say that is? Twenty feet? So the killer must have stabbed him with that funny Italian dagger—'

'A cinquedea.'

'A whatty?'

'That's what Stefano the bellboy told me. It was one of the medieval weapons displayed on the wall of the restaurant.'

'Golly. So the killer stabbed him in the back with that and then somehow hauled him over the balcony railings and sent him down there into the drink.'

Lottie gulped. It wasn't a nice thought.

'I wonder if he died from the stab wound or died from drowning?' pondered Billy. 'Awful isn't it? That poor Signor Moretti.'

'If I'd stayed out here a little longer last night, I would have witnessed it. Not a nice thought, but at least I'd have been a useful witness.' She gave the incident more thought, then added, 'I don't suppose the killer planned to murder Signor Moretti.'

'Why do you say that?' asked Billy.

'Because he took the dagger from the display on the restaurant wall. If he'd come to the hotel planning to murder him, then he'd have brought a weapon with him, don't you think? The fact he used a weapon which he found in the hotel suggests he decided at the last minute to do the deed.'

'Now, that's an interesting idea. You're suggesting he got vexed about something Signor Moretti did or said, then armed himself?'

'Or perhaps something happened which made Signor Moretti worry for his safety? So it was actually Signor Moretti who took the dagger as a precaution to defend himself with, and the attacker used it against him?'

'Another probability! You've got quite the mind, Miss Sprigg. Where do you get your ideas from?'

'I like reading detective stories. But I've not read one which has a murder like this one. I suppose I'm just trying to work out what could have happened.'

'It's certainly a puzzle,' said Billy. He looked out over the canal. 'It's a lovely view from here.' The ornate, cream buildings across the canal gleamed in the afternoon sun. 'Just like a Canaletto picture. Have you seen his paintings? He was a Venetian and painted many scenes of this city in the eighteenth century. Most of them are easily recognisable today because the city's changed so little! I bought this yesterday.' He pulled something out of his jacket and showed it to Lottie. 'A little book of his prints, pocket-sized! Isn't it delightful?' He flicked through some of the pages. 'St Mark's Square in the 1740s. Could have been painted yesterday, couldn't it? Here's a view west from the Rialto Bridge... a regatta on the Grand Canal... and this is one of my favourites because I've actually stayed at a little hotel which has this same view. This is one of the largest churches in Venice, Santi Giovanni e Paolo. Do you think I sound quite Italian when I say that name?'

'Very,' said Lottie.

They both laughed.

'What are you two chin-wagging about out there?' came Mrs Moore's voice from the room. 'The tea's arrived and I need someone to drink it with!'

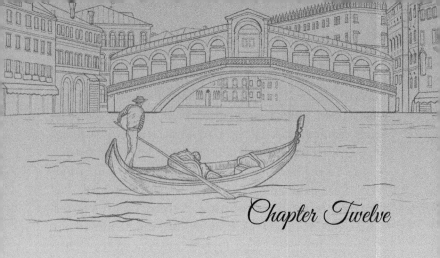

Chapter Twelve

It took Jane Harris a while to get to the other side of the canal. Having discovered that only three bridges crossed the Grand Canal, she'd had to trudge her way to the Ponte Rialto in order to get across. She could have made the crossing on a traghetto - a large gondola which took people across the canal - but she didn't like to spend money unless she really had to. And besides, the exercise was good for her.

She eventually found a location where she could observe the Grand Hotel Splendore from the other side of the canal and took a little pair of binoculars from her handbag. They'd been useful for observing the Mediterranean from the deck of a boat, and now they were proving to be even more handy. Jane adjusted the focus and trained them on the hotel balconies. A couple of guests were standing out in the sunshine.

'There's the young English girl,' she said to herself as she came across Lottie. 'And she's with that jolly, aristocratic fellow. They're in the same room together! I wonder if Mrs Moore is aware?'

She moved the binoculars along three balconies to the one

which had belonged to Signor Moretti. 'Somehow, someone managed to haul him over that balustrade,' she said. 'They must have been quite strong. Or perhaps he was already leaning against the balustrade when they attacked him? In which case, perhaps it wasn't so difficult after all.'

JANE HARRIS STOPPED at a café on her way back to the hotel and ordered a Spritz Veneziano. She'd noticed everyone seemed to drink it in Venice. It was orange, sparkling and had a refreshing bitter taste. She particularly enjoyed the fact it was served with large slices of orange.

She considered the events of the past twenty-four hours and felt relieved she'd escaped the attentions of the police so far. She'd spotted the detective talking to the pretty French lady in the lounge when she'd returned from her coffee in the piazza. Quite predictable that he'd choose the pretty ones to speak to first. It was one reason she enjoyed being older, she could float about being unremarkable and unnoticed. Youth and beauty could often be a curse.

A stooped man in tweed passed by.

'Colonel Pickering!' she called out.

He didn't seem to hear, either he was hard of hearing or he'd pretended not to notice her. 'Cooee!' she called. This time, he could pretend no longer.

'Ah, Mrs Harris.' He walked over to her. 'I didn't see you there.'

'Oh, I think you did, Colonel.'

'Really?'

'Would you like to join me for a drink?'

'Well, I...' He checked his watch, glanced around the street, then looked at her glass. 'Oh, alright then.'

He sat down and Jane called the waiter over and ordered a spritz for the colonel.

'Awful news about the opera singer chappy, isn't it?' he said.

'Terrible.'

'Did you know him at all?'

'No, the first time I spoke to him was yesterday evening when he was having dinner with that loud heiress.'

He chuckled. 'Mrs Moore? Not bad company. She's the sort of person who can be relied on to fill the gaps in conversation.'

'Fills the gaps a little too much, I fear.'

The colonel's drink arrived, and he took a large gulp. Then he examined his cufflinks and scratched at his temple. 'I suppose you're going to give me a lecture about yesterday, Mrs Harris.'

'Oh no, Colonel. I'm not the lecturing sort.'

'I sensed some disapproval on your part, though.'

'Oh dear, did my face give me away? I'm afraid there are some things I take a dim view of, but don't let that stop you doing what you enjoy.'

'Well, I do enjoy it, and I'm always careful.'

'Good. Well, that's just as well then. I hope you don't think I'm the puritanical type, I just prefer to err on the side of caution with such things.'

'Oh absolutely. Absolutely.' He took a sip of his drink. 'I can tell you're a sensible lady, Mrs Harris. You remind me a little of my wife, God rest her soul.'

'Do I really?'

'Oh yes. Very sensible she was. Kept me on the straight and narrow, that's for sure.' He took another sip. 'I miss her a great deal.'

Jane nodded, knowing only too well what widowhood felt like.

'Perhaps she's looking down on me and feels rather disappointed with what she sees.'

'Oh no, Colonel. You mustn't say such things!'

'Well, I have become a bit of a hedonist since she departed this world. Returning to the days of my youth, perhaps?' He chortled. 'I should rein it in a bit.'

'I'm sure there's no need to do that, Colonel. Just a little caution is probably all you need.'

Chapter Thirteen

ONCE BILLY HAD LEFT, Lottie sat on the balcony with her book but she found it difficult to sit still and read. After hearing Jane Harris's sleuthing story, Lottie wondered if she could find out any useful information. If she could, then she'd be able to pass it on to Commissario Romeo and hopefully distract him from the gondolier's note.

She got up from her seat and stepped back into the room. Mrs Moore had dozed off while Rosetta slept on the chaise longue. Lottie put on her sun hat and readied herself to leave. She'd almost reached the door when she felt the dog brush against her legs. 'You weren't properly asleep then?' she whispered. The dog wagged her tail in reply, and Lottie went to fetch the new lead she'd bought for her.

As they stepped outside, Lottie wondered where to go first. She decided on the opera house, reasoning that if she revisited the place, a memory of something suspicious might be jogged.

She was building a vague map of Venice in her mind and felt sure that if she followed the canal where she'd encountered the colonel, she could find her way to the opera house.

'Come along, Rosetta.' She waited as the dog tidied away a discarded ice cream cone. Although Rosetta seemed content, Lottie wondered if she missed her owner. Perhaps Rosetta was thinking he would return soon. How long would it take her to realise he wasn't coming back? This thought put a lump in Lottie's throat. The sooner the culprit was caught, the better.

A whistle from the canal made her startle. She turned to see a gondola, and steering it was the long-faced gondolier who'd given Mrs Moore the flowers. She gave him a broad grin. 'You don't know how pleased I am to see you!'

'You're pleased?' His face turned bashful.

'Oh no, I didn't mean it in that way.' His smile faded a little. 'But it's good to see you again.'

'All right. Where are you going? I can take you there.'

'That's very kind, but I don't have enough money.'

'For you, no charge.'

'That's very kind of you, but...'

'I insist.' He gestured at the velvet seat in front of him.

'Alright then, the opera house, please. Is the dog allowed?' She pointed at Rosetta.

'Of course.'

Lottie carefully lifted Rosetta into the gondola and hoped she didn't decide to jump overboard. But Rosetta seemed quite settled, perhaps Signor Moretti had taken her on boats. She made herself comfortable, and the gondolier pushed his oar into the water.

'You did not have the dog last time,' he said.

'No, I'm looking after her. She belonged to the opera singer, Amadeo Moretti. Have you heard what happened to him?'

'Of course! Everyone is talking about it.' He bent down to pass beneath a bridge.

'Sad isn't it? I need you to speak to the police for me.'

'The police? Why?'

'The commissario thinks we wrote the note which you put in the flowers.' Lottie explained what had happened to the bouquet of roses and noticed him become rather sullen.

'You gave away my gift?' he asked.

'It was Mrs Moore's idea, not mine.' She felt no guilt at putting all the blame on her employer. 'I wanted to keep them because they were lovely flowers, but we'd received an invitation at the very last moment and we didn't have time to find a gift.'

'So you gave them to Signor Moretti?'

'Yes.'

The conversation went quiet, and Lottie felt uncomfortable about asking him again to explain to Commissario Romeo that he'd written the note.

He eventually broke the silence. 'Why are you visiting the opera house?' he asked.

'I visited last night for Signor Moretti's last performance. Not that we knew it would be his last performance at the time...'

'Perhaps the murderer was there?'

'He may have been. I'm going there to jog my memory. I want to find out if I can remember anything which didn't seem right.' Such as Camille Lapointe sneaking out of Signor Moretti's dressing room. She wondered if the commissario had spoken to the French writer about it yet.

They reached the jetty at the piazza where the opera house stood. The gondolier helped her and Rosetta out. Once they were on the quayside, she said, 'I'm so sorry about the flowers, it was extremely ungrateful to give them away—'

'Please,' he interrupted. 'Don't worry about it.' He gave a broad grin. 'I have forgotten all about it now.'

'Do you mind telling Commissario Romeo you wrote the note? It will clear up the confusion.'

'Of course.'

'Thank you so much. I'm Lottie, by the way, Lottie Sprigg.'

'Vito Lombardo.' He doffed his boater hat. 'Enjoy the opera house.'

THE LARGE, heavy doors of the opera house were closed. Lottie hadn't expected them to be open, but the quiet building and the piazza in front of it looked quite different to the previous evening. Lottie sat on the steps which the glamorous guests had climbed the previous day and watched a pigeon strut along a step below her. Rosetta growled at it, then lost her patience and chased it away.

There was nothing here to jog Lottie's memory. She probably needed to go inside the opera house, but there was little chance of that. Perhaps it would remain closed as a mark of respect for Amadeo Moretti.

It was early evening now, and the tables in the piazza were filling up with people enjoying an aperitivo. The sun was low in the sky, bathing everything in a beautiful, warm glow.

'I think we wasted our time, Rosetta,' said Lottie. 'I suppose we found Vito, that was useful. And hopefully he'll explain the note to Commissario Romeo. There are no clues here, I think we should go back. It could take us a while because I'm not exactly sure of the way.'

Lottie got up and crossed the piazza.

'Rosetta!' cried out a voice. Lottie turned to see a lanky man loping towards them. He looked familiar. 'Rosetta!' he said again, crouching down to pet the dog.

Lottie remembered now where she'd seen him. 'Leporello?' It was the name of Don Giovanni's servant.

The man smiled and got to his feet. 'I'm Gustavo. You have seen the show?'

'I did. Yesterday evening. Signor Moretti invited me and my employer.'

'Ah.' His dark eyes grew damp. 'It is very sad, isn't it? He would be so grateful to know that his darling Rosetta is being cared for.'

'Yes, I intend to look after her well,' said Lottie. She looked down at the corgi and a heavy sadness weighed in her chest as she recalled she had to find a new owner for her. She turned back to Gustavo. 'Did you know Signor Moretti well?'

'Quite well. He will be sadly missed. He was always interesting.'

'In what way?'

'In many ways!' he laughed. 'If you have some time, I can tell you. Do you have some time?'

Lottie checked her watch. 'Yes, I've got about an hour.'

THEY SAT at a table outside a cafe and Gustavo ordered two Spritz Venezianos. He looked about forty and had a narrow face and expressive long-fingered hands. 'I first met Amadeo twenty years ago,' he explained. 'I had heard of him before then and so I was extremely honoured to finally meet him and share the stage with him. I was just a lowly chorus member. We were in lots of productions together and we knew each other by name and would chat occasionally. Although he was charming, he had a terrible temper, too. And he did not like anyone disagreeing with him. His ego was large and easily wounded. He was especially upset when he fell out of favour for a while.'

'What happened?'

'When we were performing Tosca at La Scala in Milan, he had an affair with the general manager's wife.'

'Oh dear.'

'Oh dear indeed. I like your funny English phrases.' He

laughed. 'So the affair meant he could never work with the general manager again which was unfortunate because the gentleman ran the greatest opera house in Italy. After that many people didn't want to work with Amadeo. For several years his name was mud, which is another funny little English phrase I like.'

'Your English is very good.'

'Thank you. I have travelled a lot in my career.'

'So Signor Moretti couldn't find work?'

'No. I am afraid to say that he turned to the drink and stopped training his voice. He made some unfortunate decisions too, I won't go into them now because I don't like to speak ill of the dead.'

'Can't you at least tell me a few of them?' ventured Lottie.

He twisted his long fingers around each other as he thought. 'Well, let's say that he fell into some bad company. It's often the way, isn't it? You drink to escape your problems and when you're under the influence of drink, you make friends with the wrong people. He actually spent a bit of time in prison.'

'Really? What for?'

'He had something to do with a bank robbery.'

'No!'

'He didn't actually do the robbery, but I think he was helping the thieves hide the money. I believe he was supposed to spend quite a long time in prison, but he had a talented lawyer and he wasn't there for long at all. He did extremely well to recover his career.'

'He did indeed. How did he manage it?'

'With the love of a good woman. She was married to someone else, but that was always the way with Amadeo, he couldn't resist other people's wives. She helped him return to his former glory. All he needed was someone to believe in him again.'

'Did the love affair last long?'

'It would have done, I'm sure. She was the one true love of his life. But sadly, she died in an automobile accident in the Alps.'

'How awful!'

'Amadeo was heartbroken, of course. But despite his heartbreak, he continued to sing. In fact, he became better than ever after her death. He said that every night he sang, he was singing for her. He liked to believe that she could hear him.'

Lottie felt her eyes growing damp. Although Signor Moretti had clearly been a rogue, the love story was moving. 'What was her name?' she asked.

'Rosetta.' He looked down at the dog, who sat by Lottie's chair. 'And that's why his beloved dog was so important to him for the rest of his days. You're doing his memory a great service by looking after her.'

Lottie finished her drink. Her mind felt light and heady now.

'Thank you very much for telling me about Signor Moretti,' she said. 'It seems he led an interesting life, and it's good to hear he mended his ways before his death.'

'I'm not sure he quite managed that.'

'Why? What did he do?'

'You realise that the character of Don Giovanni is supposed to be played by a young man? Amadeo Moretti was fifty-four years old. It surprised me when I found out he'd been cast and then I was not so surprised after all.'

'Why not?'

'Because I heard rumours he bribed the general manager to get the part. And I suspect the rumours are true.'

'He bribed him?'

'Yes. Quite typical of Amadeo, of course. I fear he was a scoundrel until the very end.'

Chapter Fourteen

LOTTIE CALLED by the kitchen when she returned to the hotel and asked for some leftovers for Rosetta. A kitchen boy was happy to oblige with some scraps of risotto and fish tails. After Rosetta had eaten her fill, Lottie took her up to the room. There was no sign of Mrs Moore.

'I wonder where she's gone?' said Lottie. 'I don't know what she's going to say when she discovers I haven't found an owner for you, Rosetta. I don't think there's any chance of me managing it today, so you'll have to stay the night.' She led the dog into her little room and wondered if there was a possibility of hiding her there. 'We could do something with these empty cases,' she said, stepping over to the pile. 'If I stack them in a certain way, I think we could make a little hidey-hole for you. You must keep nice and quiet though during the night.'

Lottie rearranged the cases and created a small area the dog could rest in without being seen from the doorway.

A knock sounded at the door and Lottie answered to find Stefano holding the laundered gowns she and Mrs Moore had worn to the opera the previous night. She thanked him and took them. 'I've just been learning more about Signor Moretti,' she said. 'Apparently, he turned to drink and spent some time in prison before making a remarkable comeback.'

'So the rumours are true? I heard he got into some trouble in the past.'

'You should have mentioned that to me sooner!'

'Should I?'

'Yes. I'm investigating his death, I need to know these things.'

'You're helping Commissario Romeo?'

'No. I'm gathering some information of my own. For Rosetta's sake, she needs justice. Did you know she's named after the only lady Amadeo Moretti truly loved?'

'No, I didn't know that.'

'If you hear anything else which you think might be useful, you'll let me know, won't you?'

'Yes. By the way, another dog has gone missing. You need to keep Rosetta safe.'

'Oh no!'

'It was a poodle. It was taken in the San Polo district, close to the Ponte Rialto.'

'How awful, I must keep a close eye on Rosetta. I don't want anybody getting their hands on her.'

'I can help you.'

'But you're so busy.'

'I will find some time. We don't want her being taken, do we?'

'No, we don't. Thank you Stefano.'

'My pleasure.' He smiled and held her gaze for a moment. 'I don't want to go, but I have to,' he said.

'You don't want to get told off by Signor Borelli.'

'No, I don't.'

. . .

LOTTIE AND ROSETTA took the dress she'd borrowed back to Madame Lapointe. 'Thank you very much for loaning it to me,' said Lottie.

'It was no problem. I don't wear it anymore, anyway. I'll fetch you the next one.'

'The next one?'

But Camille had disappeared back behind the door before Lottie could receive a reply. She returned a moment later with a beautiful three-quarter-length dress with shimmering black and gold sequins. 'Will this one do?'

'I'd never have an opportunity to wear it,' said Lottie. 'I'd love to wear it, of course, but I never go anywhere—'

'For the ball,' Madame Lapointe interrupted. 'Mrs Moore told me you need something to wear to the masquerade ball tomorrow.'

'Do I? I didn't even know I was going!'

The French lady smiled. 'Apparently so. Take it.'

'Thank you. Once again, I'm extremely grateful. I certainly don't want to be imposing on you again, borrowing your lovely clothes.'

'I don't wear this dress anymore either. It reminds me of a disastrous evening.'

'Oh no, what happened?'

'You don't need to know.'

'I suppose I probably don't.' Lottie wondered why she'd alluded to it. 'Sad news about Signor Moretti, isn't it?'

'Yes, very sad.'

'I didn't realise you knew him.'

'I didn't.'

'But I saw you yesterday evening coming out of his dressing room.'

'Impossible.'

'Oh.' Lottie wondered if she could have been mistaken. 'I felt sure it was you, never mind.'

'I hope the dress fits, I shall see you at the ball.'

'You're going too?'

'Of course. Everybody is going to the masquerade ball!'

LOTTIE AND ROSETTA had only taken a few steps along the corridor when the dog stopped to sniff something on the floor.

'What is it?' Lottie asked. She bent down to see a small, black velvet bag tied at the top with a ribbon. She picked it up and could feel something inside. Intrigued, she untied the ribbon, pulled the bag open and tipped its contents into her palm.

'Five little pebbles,' she said. 'How odd.' She put them back into the bag and tucked it into the pocket of her dress. 'I'll hand this into reception. Perhaps it means something to someone.'

'OH, THERE YOU ARE,' said Mrs Moore, when Lottie returned to the room. 'I had a nice nap then I got dressed and took a turn around the hotel. It was just as well I did because I bumped into Signor Borelli and, in the course of our conversation, I discovered the distinguished Elisabeth Contarini is hosting a masquerade ball at the Palazzo Sacrati tomorrow evening. And you will never guess who's attending!'

'Everyone I'm told.'

'Where did you hear that? It's not the sort of event which everyone goes to, only a select few. Anyway, I've secured us an invitation because Prince Manfred of Bavaria will be there!' She beamed and clapped her hands together in excitement. 'I shall go to great lengths to ensure that I dance with him tomorrow. Won't that be something? Now I see our French friend has loaned you a dress for the evening. Hold it up for me so I can have a proper look.' Lottie did so. 'Rather sparkly isn't it? A little ostentatious if you ask me, but that's French fashion for you. Hopefully you won't stand out too much, a lot of people will be dressed in costume at the ball. We need to wear masks! Isn't that exciting? We can go on a little shopping expedition tomorrow to buy some. Oh, it's going to be so much fun!'

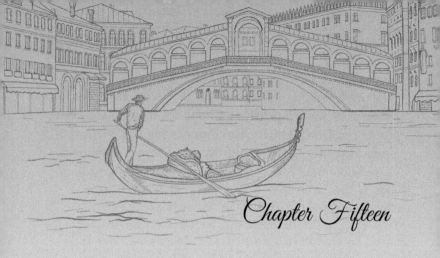

Chapter Fifteen

THE MASQUERADE BALL! Billy was looking forward to it enormously. It was a chance to dress up! He headed for the shopping district of Le Mercerie just as the shops were opening for the day. He was after a Pierrot outfit: a baggy white suit with large pom pom buttons. He'd been drawn to Pierrot ever since he'd seen the character in a pantomime as a boy.

He called in at a costume shop and was delighted to discover an elaborate Pierrot costume with a fancy neck ruff and a white mask with arched eyebrows and red rosebud lips.

'You really want to be Pierrot?' asked the shopkeeper.

'Yes!'

'Not Harlequin?' He pulled a chequered suit of red, gold and green off the rail and held it up. 'Harlequin is clever and witty! And most important of all, he is irresistible to Columbina. She rejects Pierrot for him! Which is not surprising, because Pierrot is just a sad clown. You want to be a sad clown?'

'Yes!' said Billy. 'Can I try on the costume?'

'If you wish.' The shopkeeper gestured at the curtained-off changing cubicle.

ONCE HE'D HIRED the costume, Billy bounced along in the sunshine looking for a cafe to stop at for coffee. He reached the Grand Canal and paused for a moment, watching the boats. He loved the fact Venice had no traffic. No noisy motor cars charging about or dirty, smelly roads to cross. Venice was a place which lived in a time of its own. How wonderful it must have been to live here when it had been a wealthy republic of its own ruled by the Doge. What times those must have been! It wasn't difficult to look at the old buildings and streets and imagine wealthy merchants and Venetian nobility swanning about in their colourful clothes.

Up ahead was the Ponte Rialto, spanning the canal and gleaming white in the morning sunshine. He climbed the steps of the bridge, always busy with people browsing the shops or admiring the view. On the bridge itself were several pretty little shops. He paused by a jeweller's window and peered in at the necklaces and rings. What he really needed was a lady to buy them for.

He became aware of an old lady in a pink hat alongside him. He turned and realised he recognised her. 'Mrs Harris?' he asked. 'From the Grand Hotel Splendore?'

She gave a wide smile. 'Yes, that's me alright. Call me Jane. You're Billy, aren't you?'

'That's right. Beautiful morning for a bit of shopping, isn't it?'

'It certainly is, although just window shopping for me. I can't afford half of these lovely things. Instead, I just admire them through the window.'

'The best type of shopping,' he said. 'You spend much less that way.' They both laughed.

'I've just hired my costume for the masquerade ball this evening at Palazzo Sacrati. Please tell me you're coming too?'

'I hadn't heard of it until you mentioned it just now.'

'You must come! I'll get you an invitation. The host is Signora Elisabeth Contarini, apparently she's descended from a Venetian noble.'

'She sounds interesting indeed.'

'Doesn't she? You need a mask.'

'Do I?'

'Yes! It's a masquerade ball, we're not supposed to know who anyone is.'

'Golly.'

'Isn't it going to be fun when we don't know who anyone is? We can play tricks on people!'

'Well, I'll leave the tricks to you, Billy, but I'll happily wear a mask. Can we invite Colonel Pickering too? He was looking rather sorry for himself at breakfast this morning.'

'Absolutely. The more the merrier!'

Chapter Sixteen

'How do I look?' Mrs Moore held the colourful mask over her eyes and gave a loud laugh.

'Ravishing,' said Lottie. The mask was gold and jewelled with a fan of large blue feathers attached to one side.

'Are you pleased with yours, Lottie?'

'Very pleased.' She had chosen a red, black and gold mask to match the dress she'd been lent. The lady in the shop had told them they were Columbina masks and that the name came from the character of a maid in the traditional Italian commedia dell'arte plays.

'I wonder what mask Prince Manfred is wearing,' mused Mrs Moore, picking up her coffee cup. 'There are lots of different styles to choose from, aren't there? There's... Harlequin, I remember that one. What are the others?'

'Pulcinella I think. Then there's Volto, Scaramouche, Pierrot, Bauta and Gatto, which is the cat. There's the plague doctor mask too.' Lottie shuddered at this one, remembering Stefano's description of the masked figure who roamed Venice at night.

'What a memory you have for detail, Lottie. It's because

you're young, I suppose. My brain worked like that when I was young. The trouble with getting older is you have more important things to dwell on. It means the small, irrelevant details are quickly forgotten.'

They had spent all morning shopping, and Lottie feared they would be doing it all afternoon too. There was little time to work on her investigation and she was worried about Rosetta being left on her own. Amidst the excitement, Mrs Moore appeared to have forgotten about the dog for the time being. Fortunately, Rosetta had kept quiet in her makeshift den overnight, and Lottie had sneaked her a bit of bacon and bread from breakfast. Rosetta needed to get outside, though.

'Where shall we have lunch?' said Mrs Moore. 'I overheard someone in the hotel lounge talking about a place they'd enjoyed, but I can't remember what it was called now. We passed a nice-looking place on the way here, didn't we? Now, where was that again?'

'Just off St Mark's Square.'

'Oh, that's right. It might be worth trying.'

Lottie had to get back to the hotel, if only for a brief while. She formulated a plan as she finished her coffee.

'You've accumulated a lot of bags and boxes, Mrs Moore, how about I take these back to the hotel while you think about where to have lunch?'

'Oh, don't worry about that, Lottie. It's a bit of a walk.'

'I don't think it will take me any longer than fifteen minutes to get there.'

'It will take you fifteen minutes to get there, five minutes to take everything up to the room... get that bellboy friend of yours to help you. Then another fifteen minutes to get back... Wait, that's thirty minutes! Actually, it's thirty-five! I can't sit here on my own for that long!'

'Why not order another coffee? And perhaps an ice cream to go with it?'

'Now there's a thought.'

'This table is in a splendid position, you can watch everyone passing by. You usually enjoy that, don't you?'

'I suppose so.'

'And if I have to lug these bags around all afternoon, I won't be able to carry anything else if you decide to do more shopping.'

'That would be a shame. Alright then, off you go. But no longer than thirty-five minutes! Run if you have to!'

As soon as she was back at the hotel, Lottie dashed up to the room. Rosetta jumped down from her bed and wagged her tail. 'I can take you out, but only for two minutes!' said Lottie, checking her watch.

She walked Rosetta around the piazza as quickly as possible, then returned to the hotel. Stefano was pushing a heavily laden luggage trolley across the lobby.

'Hello Lottie!'

'Hello. You have to help me with Rosetta today. Mrs Moore's taken me on an awful all-day shopping trip and I'm unable to keep Rosetta company.'

'Well neither am I.'

'I thought you said you could help?'

'I can, but Signor Borelli's keeping a close eye on me at the moment. He's accused me of not working hard enough.'

'I'm sorry to hear it. Can you find five minutes here and there to check on her and maybe take her outside?'

'I'll try. But—'

'Do you often get asked to mind guest's dogs?'

'Sometimes.'

'So just tell Signor Borelli that's what you're doing! Rosetta doesn't need much, and I'd be extremely grateful, I really would. But you have to keep it quiet from Mrs

Moore because she doesn't know I'm still looking after her.'

'What?' He laughed. 'You're going to have to tell her!'

'I realise that.'

'How are you keeping her secret?'

'I don't know. I didn't intend it to be this way, but it's the situation I've found myself in.'

'Alright then, hand her to me.' He reached out and took the lead.

'Thank you Stefano. How can I repay you?'

'There's no need. Consider it a favour for a friend.'

LOTTIE MADE her way back to the café. On her way, she mused over the story of Amadeo Moretti's criminal past. Assisting bank robbers and receiving a prison sentence didn't sound good. Neither did bribing the general manager of the opera house so he could have the part of Don Giovanni. But were the misdemeanours the reason he'd been murdered? Although it was easy to think so, perhaps it was too obvious.

Her thoughts distracted her, and she took a wrong turn. Certain that she could correct herself, she took another few turns, then found herself in a narrow, dingy street away from the shoppers and tourists. There were no shops or cafes here, just rows of little doorways and shuttered windows.

The street opened out into a little square dominated by a sombre, grey church. An austere building occupied another side of the square, it looked as though it served an administrative purpose. A cool breeze whisked around the empty piazza, blowing dead leaves into a whirlpool. Narrow streets led away from each corner of the square. Which one should she take?

An old, bent lady trudged across the square with a little dog in tow. 'Excuse me!' Lottie called out to her, but she appeared not to hear. 'Hello!' The old woman turned in her direction and Lottie gave a gasp when she saw the old lady's eyes were clouded with white. With no sign that she wished to talk or stop, the old lady exited the square at the far corner, her dog following behind.

Lottie felt her stomach twist with horror. She needed to get back to the busy streets. Not wishing to follow the sinister lady, she took off across the square and chose a street to dash down. It ended at a narrow canal. A dead end. She turned, ran back to the square and reluctantly followed the route the old lady had taken.

This street was no cheerier, but at least it wasn't a dead end like the last one had been. It ended at a bridge. Lottie slowed her pace, not wishing to catch up with the sinister lady.

Lottie stopped on the bridge. She was now above a narrow canal and there was a dank odour in the air. The other side of the bridge led to a passage with a dark archway. It must have been where the old lady had gone, and it seemed to lead even further from the safety and bustle of the city.

Lottie felt a prickle on the back of her neck.

She turned to go back and was confronted with a figure which suddenly withdrew into shadow.

It had moved swiftly out of sight, but Lottie had seen enough. For a brief second, she'd seen the long, hooked nose of the plague doctor mask.

She gave a shriek and headed for the dark archway.

Chapter Seventeen

RUNNING AS FAST as she could, Lottie headed for the end of the dark passageway, her heart thudding in her ears. There was no sound of footsteps behind her, but she dared not turn and look. To her immediate joy, the passageway opened out into a busy shopping street. Lottie laughed with relief as she stumbled her way through the crowds, recovering her breath. Suddenly, it seemed silly to have been so frightened. Perhaps her imagination had got the better of her and the masked figure hadn't been there at all? She shook her head to bring herself to her senses and recognised the shop where she and Mrs Moore had bought their masks. A moment later, she was back at the café.

Mrs Moore had company. Colonel Pickering. He got to his feet and gave a bow as Lottie approached.

'You've met the colonel, haven't you, Lottie?' asked Mrs Moore.

'I certainly have.' He gave her a nod, but there was a hard glint in his eye as if warning her not to mention the money she'd seen him drop. His tie was patterned with stripes and an insignia which denoted membership of an organisation.

Perhaps it was connected with his military service or a gentleman's club.

'We've been discussing recent events, haven't we, Colonel?' said Mrs Moore. 'Apparently, the police won't leave him alone.'

'I'm sorry to hear it,' said Lottie. She knew she wouldn't be sorry if he turned out to be the murderer, but she had to be polite for now.

'Darned nuisance, it is. It's because I was the last person to see him alive.'

'At the bar?'

'Yes, at the bar and...' He scratched his nose. 'I'm afraid to say I went to Mr Moretti's room as well. He wanted to show me some old medals he'd bought in an auction. I wasn't there for long, but you know how it looks. Shortly afterwards, the chap was skewered with a medieval knife and deposited in the canal. Dreadful business.'

Although he looked no younger than seventy, he was well built and had broad shoulders. Lottie wondered if he had the strength to lift the opera singer over the balcony railings.

'He probably had an argument with someone,' continued the colonel. 'I heard he had a temper, not that I witnessed it myself.'

'When did you first meet him?' Lottie asked.

'Just a few days ago! I didn't know him well, but he liked to stay up late in the hotel bar, as do I. I struggle to get to sleep much before the early hours these days. I can't imagine it was good for his voice staying up late like that, he enjoyed a drink too. But he seems to have got by alright. Highly thought of, wasn't he?'

'He was indeed,' said Mrs Moore.

'He reminded me of a chap I was at Sandhurst with. That chap wasn't Italian, though. Moretti appeared to have done a few interesting things in his time, not all of them suitable to mention in the presence of ladies, I should add.'

'Oh dear!' Mrs Moore frowned. 'And to think he was a distinguished opera singer.'

'But flesh and blood, just like the next man, I'm afraid. With all the desires and urges that entails.'

'Thank you, Colonel,' snapped Mrs Moore. 'I don't think we need to hear any more on that front.'

'Did you see anyone else near Signor Moretti's room that evening, Colonel?' asked Lottie.

'You sound just like one of those police officers!' He chortled. 'No, I didn't. Baffling isn't it? We had a drink or two at the bar and he was bending my ear about those medals, I think they were from the Napoleonic Wars or something like that. People often assume I'm interested in old war memorabilia because I'm a military man. And while I can't deny that I harbour some interest in it, I can't say that I'm interested enough to be dawdling about examining medals in some chap's room at midnight. Anyway, I thought I should go just to keep the man quiet and prevent him from introducing the topic again the following evening. As it turned out, there was no following evening, was there?'

'What time was that?'

'About a quarter to midnight.'

'How long were you in his room for?' asked Lottie.

He chuckled again. 'You fancy yourself as a little detective, don't you, young lady?' She bristled at the word "little". 'I don't think it was more than ten minutes. Just long enough to examine the aforementioned medals and make general signs of being impressed by them and that sort of thing. I think he wanted me to assure him they were worth more than he'd paid for them.'

'And were they?' asked Mrs Moore.

'No idea. I'm a retired colonel, not an auctioneer.'

'So you were in his room for about ten minutes, then left,' said Lottie. 'And when you left, did you notice anyone else in the corridor?'

'Only a maid. She was carrying a tray to one of the rooms. I bid her goodnight, she was pleasant enough.'

'That means she was in the corridor close to the time of Signor Moretti's murder,' said Lottie. 'I wonder if she saw anything suspicious?'

'You'd have to ask her that.'

'What did she look like?'

'A maid. Apron, cap, that sort of thing. Quite plump. Brown hair and spectacles. I say she was a girl, but she was a woman, really. Anyway...' he checked his watch. 'I must be off, I'm meeting a friend for lunch. Delightful to see you both.'

'Will we see you at the masquerade ball this evening, Colonel?'

'Oh yes, I've been invited by Jane Harris,' he said. 'After lunch I shall go and find a costume!'

'THE MAID MUST HAVE SEEN or heard something,' said Lottie as they watched the colonel walk away. 'I wonder if Commissario Romeo's spoken to her?'

'Which maid?' asked Mrs Moore.

'The maid the colonel saw when he left Signor Moretti's room.'

'Oh her. I must say that I agree with the colonel describing you as a little detective. You can't get too nosy, you know. It's not good manners.'

Chapter Eighteen

THAT EVENING, a short gondola ride brought Lottie and Mrs Moore to a jetty at the Palazzo Sacrati. It was a terracotta building with pointed arch windows. Many guests were arriving by boat and they had to wait their turn to disembark.

'That dress fits you well, Lottie.' Mrs Moore examined her through her lorgnette.

'Thank you.' Lottie felt pleased with how her outfit sparkled in the early evening light. She'd borrowed another pair of Mrs Moore's silk gloves and a gold beaded headband. She clutched her mask in her hand, too shy to wear it until they got out of the gondola.

Mrs Moore was resplendent in a voluminous gown coloured like a peacock's tail. The wide skirts filled the width of the gondola, and Lottie imagined it was going to take a while to extricate her employer from the boat.

As they bobbed on the water, Lottie watched the other guests climb out of their gondolas and make their way up the grand steps of the palace. Their costumes were a riot of colour: jackets and dresses in velvet and silk and trimmed with lace and gold braid. Large hats and wigs were decorated with ribbons, beads and flowers. Sequins shimmered and large ostrich feathers wafted in the warm evening breeze. And everyone wore masks: some covered just the eyes while others covered the entire face.

A masked lady greeted the guests at the top of the steps. In her white powdered wig and silk blue gown frothed with lace and bows, she had the appearance of Marie Antoinette.

'That's Signora Contarini,' said Mrs Moore. 'She's very rich. Let's put on our masks.'

SIGNORA CONTARINI WAS perfunctory in her handshake, she had a lot of guests to greet. After their brief welcome, Lottie and Mrs Moore were ushered into a busy entrance hall with marble columns and ornate plasterwork. They followed the strains of music into a ballroom with tall windows and chandeliers which hung from the ceiling on giant brass chains. In the centre of the ceiling, a fresco depicted a God-like figure riding through the clouds on a golden chariot. On the dance-floor, guests whirled dangerously close to priceless urns and statues positioned on plinths along the walls.

On the far wall, Lottie spotted a balcony with an elaborate balustrade. The position afforded a bird's eye view of the dancers and a handful of people stood there now. A plump, moustachioed man in a shimmering orange frock coat caught her eye. He wore an enormous bow of lace at his neck and his gold mask covered his eyes and nose. His costume gave him the appearance of an eighteenth-century dandy.

'I spy him!' said Mrs Moore, peering at him through her lorgnette. 'Prince Manfred of Bavaria! He shall be choosing which ladies to dance with. I must make sure I catch his eye!'

And with that, she disappeared into the colourful throng.

Lottie was happy to stand at the side of the room and marvel at the costumes of the masked dancers as they passed her by. A lady dressed like a Tudor queen, a man in a three-cornered hat and matching velvet cloak, a Harlequin clown with diamonds of red, gold and green, and even a lady with a birdcage as a headdress. Was the little songbird in it real?

'Boo!' A Pierrot clown joined her and lifted his mask to reveal a shiny, red face. 'Only me!' he said.

'Hello Billy,' said Lottie. 'You're enjoying yourself?'

'Immensely! I don't think I've ever been to a party as glamorous as this before, have you?'

'Never.' Lottie was still struggling to take it all in.

'Where's Mrs Moore?'

'She's trying to get a dance with Prince Manfred.'

'Is she now?' Billy chuckled. 'Then she'd better join the queue. I've heard he's the second most eligible bachelor in Europe.'

'Who's the first?'

'Why me, of course!'

Lottie laughed.

'What's so funny?' he said. 'It's true! Alright then, I admit it isn't. I can't tell you how envious I am of him. Wouldn't it be wondrous to be born into royalty? Even though the Bavarian king was deposed at the end of the war, old Manfred looks like he still gets to have a good time, doesn't he?' They watched as the prince and his assistants left the balcony. 'Prepare yourselves ladies!' said Billy. 'Prince Manfred is on his way!'

Jane Harris joined them. She wore a pink silk gown and held a white and pink mask on a stick. 'Who are we talking about?' she asked.

'Prince Manfred,' said Billy.

'Who's he?'

'You should have been here two minutes ago, we can't be bothered to repeat ourselves now.'

'What a cheeky young man you are, Billy.'

'Prince Manfred of Bavaria is the most eligible bachelor in Europe,' said Lottie.

'Second,' said Billy.

'I think I might go into the salon,' said Jane. 'It's rather noisy in here.'

'I'll come with you,' said Lottie.

'I'm staying here,' said Billy, 'I'm going to find someone to dance with.'

LOTTIE ACCOMPANIED Jane to the salon at the side of the main ballroom. It was laid out as a lounge, with groups of elegant chairs and low tables.

'This is better,' said Jane, taking a seat. 'There's a bit of air here from the balcony.' A pair of tall doors stood open, framed by a pair of heavy brocade curtains.

'How long has Prince Manfred been Europe's most eligible bachelor for?' Jane asked Lottie.

'I don't know.'

'Because if he's been a bachelor for a long time, surely he can't be that eligible?'

'Why not?'

'It must mean there's something wrong with him.'

'That's a good point.'

'I was always wary of men who had been bachelors for a long time. I could only imagine that the ladies courting them had found a good reason not to marry them.'

'Perhaps Prince Manfred has only recently become a bachelor?'

'What was he doing before?'

'I don't know. That's an interesting question.'

Lottie wondered for a moment what would happen to her if Mrs Moore married him. She pictured a future working in a Bavarian castle. Although the thought was exciting, she wouldn't like to do it forever. She felt sure she'd get homesick.

'HAVEN'T WE MET SOMEWHERE BEFORE?' said a man in a military costume. He wore a red and gold braided jacket and silk breeches with long leather boots. A fluffy white ostrich feather was stuck into his velvet hat and he wore a plain black mask over his eyes.

'Colonel Pickering!' Jane giggled. 'You look very distinguished. Is that a real sword?'

'It's a decorative one.' He glanced down at the long sheath which hung from the side of his belt. 'Probably no good in a proper sword fight. I'm not usually one for dressing up, but I must say that I'm rather enjoying it. Now, which of you lovely ladies would like the pleasure of a dance?'

'Oh not me,' said Jane. 'I've got a bone in my leg.'

'Hasn't everyone?'

'Yes, but it still sounds like a good excuse, don't you think?'

'It's an excellent one! Miss Sprigg?'

'Erm...' Lottie felt her cheeks flush with shame. 'I'm afraid I can't dance, Colonel.' It wasn't a skill she'd ever been taught at the orphanage. She waited for the colonel to walk away.

'That doesn't matter at all!' he said.

'But it does. I'll embarrass myself!'

'No one will care,' he said. 'Most of these dances are a simple waltz, you just need the box step for that.'

'It sounds complicated.'

'It's not.' He gave a little demonstration. 'Walk, side, close. Walk, side, close. That's all you do. Ad infinitum. Let's give it a try.' He held out his hand.

'Go on,' said Jane.

'Oh alright,' said Lottie, taking the colonel's hand.

. . .

IN THE BALLROOM, they took up their position among the dancers. The orchestra played a little introduction, then they were off. After bumping into the colonel a few times and stepping on his toes, Lottie managed a half-decent box step as they made their way around the room.

'I should say thank you for not mentioning our little meeting by the canal to anyone,' he said.

'What meeting was that?'

'Ah ha! Very good, that's my girl.'

'Do you mean when I helped you pick up the money?' Lottie hadn't considered it a meeting.

'Yes. That's the one. People would take a dim view if they knew about it, so thank you for keeping it all hush-hush.'

'That's alright.' She'd mentioned it to Stefano, but she hoped the colonel was less worried about a bellboy finding out and more concerned about people such as Mrs Moore or Commissario Romeo. She hadn't mentioned it to Mrs Moore because she felt sure she'd gossip about it. But why didn't he want other people to find out about it? Was he up to something suspicious?

'I've done nothing wrong, by the way,' he added, as if reading her mind. 'It's all completely above board, but if there's one thing that gets people gossiping, it's money.'

'I agree, Colonel.'

In a flash of orange, Prince Manfred whirled by. He was dancing with a lady in canary yellow and not Mrs Moore. She spotted her employer a short while later dancing with Billy.

At the end of the dance, the colonel thanked her with a polite bow. 'These costumes are dreadfully hot, aren't they?' he said. 'I'm going to get a bit of air now and then I'm going to invite that charming French lady to dance.'

'Madame Lapointe?'

'That's the one. She promised me a dance earlier and I'm holding her to it.'

LOTTIE WAS happy to watch the dancing again, although the eyeholes of her mask limited her view a little. For the next song, the prince had swapped to a lady in lime green and Mrs Moore danced with a highwayman. Billy had found the lady with the birdcage on her head.

Lottie smiled as they passed her by, but a chill ran through her when she caught sight of another dancer. A plague doctor in a white hook-nosed mask, black cape and wide-brimmed hat.

She told herself it was just someone having fun in a costume. But there was something about him which gave her the shivers. As he passed, she caught the glint of his eyes in the dark holes of his mask.

Lottie quivered. Perhaps she was overreacting?

No, she wasn't. As the plague doctor moved away, his macabre mask remained fixed in her direction.

Chapter Nineteen

LOTTIE COULDN'T BEAR the scrutiny of the plague doctor's gaze. She left the ballroom and made her way to the ladies' powder room.

Inside, ladies preened themselves in front of large mirrors. Lottie adjusted her headband and her gaze caught the black-edged eyes of someone familiar.

'Madame Lapointe. How are you?'

'I've been better.' The French writer was dressed in red silk and sequins. She gazed sadly at something in her hands. 'My mask is broken.'

'Oh no. What a shame!'

It was a Gatto cat mask with two small ears and was beautifully decorated in black, red, and gold. Made of papier mâché, like many masks, it was cracked in the centre and had almost separated in two. 'The ribbon came undone,' said Madame Lapointe. 'It fell off and, before I could pick it up again, that oversized Bavarian prince stepped on it.'

'I hope he apologised!'

'Yes, he did. It was an accident. But it also means I have no mask for the rest of the evening, I shall have to go back to the hotel.'

'No! Surely you can enjoy the ball without a mask?'

'But it's a masked ball! Everyone must look mysterious. I don't want to be the only person without a mask.'

Lottie noticed their masks were similar colours and that hers would match Madame Lapointe's dress. 'Take mine,' she said, untying it.

'No, I couldn't possibly.'

'Please.' Lottie held it out to her. 'I've just had a dance and I won't be doing another, I've got two left feet.'

'Really?'

'It was a joke.'

'Oh, of course.' Madame Lapointe gave an embarrassed smile at her mistake.

'Please take it,' said Lottie. 'You've lent me two dresses, so this is my return favour. And besides, Colonel Pickering says you've promised him a dance.'

She smiled. 'I have indeed. He's a charming gentleman, isn't he? Quite an English eccentric. This is very kind of you. I shall wear it for just a few dances and then I can return it to you.'

'Wear it for the rest of the evening if you like, I don't mind.'

Madame Lapointe dropped her broken mask into the wastepaper basket and tied on the new one. Then she admired herself in the mirror.

'Beautiful,' said Lottie.

As LOTTIE LEFT the powder room, she caught sight of the plague doctor hurrying across the entrance hall to the main door. It stood open after admitting the evening's guests. Lottie tucked herself behind a column and watched him leave.

He paused at the top of the steps, his cloak billowing in the evening breeze. Then he descended the steps and disappeared into the night. Lottie skipped to the entrance and peeked out from behind one of the large heavy doors. The steps led down to the jetty and the canal. The only way the man could leave was by boat. Perhaps he would take off his mask after leaving the building and Lottie could see who he was?

But all she could see outside were the lights of Venice reflected in the canal. Cautiously, Lottie moved out to the top of the steps. There was no one else around.

From the inky black canal came the sound of an oar dipping into water. The plague doctor must have found a waiting gondola. It must have been a stroke of luck because she couldn't see any others waiting. She imagined gondoliers would congregate here later to take guests home, the night was presumably too young for people to leave yet.

A bell struck ten and Lottie wondered why the masked man had left early. If he was the same man who'd been prowling the streets and canals at night, why hadn't someone confronted him? Was he the dog snatcher? It felt too puzzling.

Lottie remained on the steps for a while, breathing in the evening air. She relished the tranquillity of this moment with the strains of a waltz in the background accompanied by the chatter and laughter of people enjoying themselves.

Then everything fell silent.

It was as though time had stopped. Nothing moved except the ripples of light on the canal.

Lottie held her breath and a breeze chilled her shoulders.

Something seemed wrong.

She turned and made her way back up the steps.

.   .   .

IN THE ENTRANCE HALL, people either stood in silence or talked in low voices. The party mood had evaporated. She felt a heavy lurch in her stomach and went into the ballroom, where the dancing had stopped and people huddled in groups. Some people had removed their masks, and she saw a lady weeping.

'Oh Lottie, there you are!' cried out Mrs Moore, dashing towards her.

'What's happened?'

'It's Colonel Pickering. He's dead!'

Chapter Twenty

'He was in the salon,' said Mrs Moore. 'He was stabbed in the back!'

'Surely someone witnessed it?' said Lottie.

'It happened behind a curtain. He must have been pushed behind it and then stabbed! They can't find anyone who witnessed it. Someone noticed his feet poking out beneath the curtain and they assumed he was drunk. But then they pulled back the curtain and saw him lying face down with a sword in his back.'

'Not the sword from his costume?'

'It must have been.'

'But why?' she said. 'I don't understand!'

'Me neither,' said Mrs Moore.

'I danced with him just a short while ago, and then Madame Lapointe was going to find him for a dance. Everything seemed fine. He was having a good time.' Lottie felt tears rush to her eyes. Police officers began ushering people into the ballroom, away from the salon.

Lottie tried to imagine how the murder had come about. Had the colonel shown the sword to someone who'd then grabbed it and attacked him? If so, then how had they plunged it into his back? She wondered if the colonel had been standing with his back to his assailant and they'd crept up behind him, carefully pulled out the sword and carried out the attack before he could do anything about it. But why hadn't someone else noticed?

As everyone was told to wait in the ballroom, Lottie realised how lucky it was for the plague doctor that he'd got away. Surely he had to be the murderer?

AFTER A POOR NIGHT'S SLEEP, Lottie woke early and sneaked outside with Rosetta while Mrs Moore slept. She saw Stefano in the lobby, pushing a trolley.

'I heard about Colonel Pickering!' he said in a hushed voice. 'Did you see what happened?'

'No, I was outside on the palazzo steps at the time. Then I heard the music stop, I went back inside and found out what had happened. I can't believe it!'

'Why would someone murder the colonel?'

'I don't know! It's terrible. I danced with him not long before it happened.'

'How was he?'

'He was happy. His normal self.' Lottie felt a lump in her throat. She gave a swallow and continued. 'We had a dance together, and he thanked me for not mentioning the money to anyone.'

'You mentioned it to me.'

'I know, but I trust you.'

He grinned. 'Thank you.'

'I didn't tell anyone else, though. And the fact that he didn't want people to know about it suggests it could have been something criminal, doesn't it? I think he had something to hide.'

'It sounds like it,' said Stefano.

'There's no use in me keeping the colonel's money quiet anymore, is there? It could be the reason he was murdered.'

'And it has to be the same person who murdered Signor Moretti, don't you think? Two similar murders in just two days?'

'I think so,' said Lottie. 'So there's the question of what links Amadeo Moretti and the colonel. Did they have a common enemy? Who was it? The two had a drink together the evening before Amadeo's death. I wish we could find out what they were talking about.'

'I'll ask Angelo.'

'Who's that?'

'The barman who was working that night. He might have overheard something, he has a good understanding of English.'

'That would be brilliant,' said Lottie. 'There's something else I need to tell you, too. I saw the plague doctor at the ball last night!'

'No!'

'Yes! And he left around the time Colonel Pickering was murdered. I think I saw him just after he committed the murder!'

'Have you told the police yet?'

'Not yet.'

'Commissario Romeo's in the lounge. Tell him now.'

'I will. Thank you for looking after Rosetta yesterday.'

'No problem. Have you told Mrs Moore that you're keeping her now?'

'No. I can't keep her, can I? I'm not allowed to.'

'So what will happen when she finds the dog in your room?'

'I don't know. I don't want to think about it. I'll find the courage to tell her later today. So much has happened, it's difficult to find the time.'

'Stefano!' Signor Borelli marched into the lobby.

'I've got to go.'

LOTTIE WENT into the lounge with Rosetta and spotted the commissario sitting in a cloud of tobacco smoke with his bespectacled deputy. The two men were in deep discussion, but the commissario gestured to an empty chair as he saw Lottie approach.

'I'm keen to speak with you,' he said.

'Are you?' Lottie didn't like the steeliness in his dark grey eyes. She perched on the chair and noted four empty espresso cups on the table, the police clearly needed a lot of coffee today.

The commissario pointed his floppy little cigarette at her. 'You were seen dancing with Colonel Pickering shortly before his death,' he said.

'Yes, that's right. He danced with a few people. I need to tell you about—'

'All in good time.' He held up his hand to stop her. 'What did you discuss as you danced?'

Lottie thought it best to be as honest as possible. 'We talked about some money which he dropped yesterday morning. I helped him pick it up.'

'Money? How much money?'

'I don't know exactly, but it was quite a lot because it was in five hundred lire notes.'

'Five hundred lire?'

'I think there could have been fifty or sixty of them.'

Commissario Romeo gave a little whistle of surprise.

'So it could have been between twenty-five to thirty thousand lire.'

The commissario made a note. 'That's a lot of money. Where did he get it from?'

'I don't know. He didn't want anyone to know because he said people could get funny about it and gossip.'

'Do you know what he was doing with the money?'

'He told me he was going to the bank.'

'Do you know which one?'

'No.'

He made some more notes, then sucked on his cigarette. 'So you danced with Colonel Pickering and talked about the money. Did you talk about anything else?'

'No, that was all.'

'And was that the last time you saw him?'

'Yes. He was planning to dance with Camille Lapointe afterwards.'

'The French writer?' He gave a slight smile. 'Very interesting. Do you know if they danced together?'

'I didn't see them dancing together, but I can't see why they wouldn't have. I saw Madame Lapointe in the powder room just before she went to dance with him.'

'And what time was that?'

'It was almost ten o'clock. And then, after that, I saw—'

He held up his hand again. 'Allow me to guide the conversation, Miss Sprigg.'

Lottie felt a snap of impatience in her chest. 'But I saw—'

'We will discuss it next. Okay? Now it is interesting that you danced with Colonel Pickering shortly before his death. It is also interesting that you gave Signor Moretti a note about falling into the canal. Is it just a coincidence that you met with both men shortly before they were murdered?'

'Yes!' She held his gaze, desperate for him to believe her. But as she did so, her face heated up. He'd probably notice the redness and assume she was lying. The more she tried to convince him, the guiltier she seemed. 'Has Vito Lombardo spoken to you yet?' she asked.

'No. Who's he?'

'The gondolier who wrote the note about falling into the canal. I found him and asked him to speak to you.'

'Then I shall look forward to it.'

Lottie wished Vito would hurry up and tell the commissario the truth. But he had no incentive to do so and was probably still offended they'd given his gift away.

Commissario Romeo glanced down at Rosetta, then smiled and patted her on the head. 'You still have Signor Moretti's dog.'

'Yes, I'm looking after her for the time being.'

'Interesting.'

Lottie wondered why it was interesting. Was it something else he would use against her?

'Now what were you going to tell me?' he asked. 'You mentioned you saw something?'

'Yes! The plague doctor.'

'Who's he?'

'The one who wanders about at night. I saw him...' She trailed off as she noticed him laughing. 'What's funny?'

'You realise he's not real? Someone seems to have invented a story of a man who wears a mask and cape and steals dogs.'

'But everybody's worried about the dog snatcher! Yesterday I heard a poodle was taken in the San Polo district.'

'Yes, yes. Someone is having a very good joke at the moment. You say you saw the plague doctor? And this one was real?'

'Yes. At the ball last night. He left just before Colonel Pickering was found dead. He got away.'

'You think this man dressed as the plague doctor is the murderer?' he said.

'I don't know for sure. But I know he left alone before

anyone else. I think he must have been making his getaway. And there was something strange about him.'

'Which was what?'

'I saw him dancing, and he kept looking at me.'

'You're a pretty young lady, why shouldn't he look at you?'

Lottie clenched her teeth. What did she have to do to make this man take her seriously? 'I don't mean like that,' she snapped. 'There was something sinister about it.'

'There *is* something sinister about a plague doctor's mask. I would feel uncomfortable about a man in a plague doctor mask staring at me, too. Even more uncomfortable than you, Miss Sprigg!' He turned to his deputy, and they both laughed.

Lottie got to her feet, anger balled in her chest. 'I have to go now.'

'Thank you for your time, Signorina.'

Chapter Twenty-One

Lottie instructed Rosetta to wait in the corridor before she went into the hotel room. Inside, Mrs Moore was awake but still in bed. 'It's all too much,' she moaned. 'All too much, I tell you. The colonel's murder has brought on another one of my headaches.'

'I'm sorry to hear it, I'll fetch the Stark's.'

'Please inform Signor Borelli.'

'The hotel manager?'

'Yes. Then he can tell his staff to keep away. A maid has already disturbed me returning our laundered gowns from last night.'

'They've been laundered already?'

'Apparently so, and I can't tell you how loudly the maid knocked on the door. It was deafening. Where were you?'

'I was being interviewed by Commissario Romeo.'

'Oh dear, again? Then you really must tell Signor Borelli I'm unwell, I couldn't possibly face that police inspector again.'

· · ·

LOTTIE RETURNED the dress she'd worn the previous night to Camille Lapointe. This time, Madame Lapointe invited her and Rosetta into the room rather than talking through the gap in the door. Lottie wondered if this gesture of friendliness was because she'd lent her the mask at the ball.

Madame Lapointe clearly liked flowers, there were vases of them arranged around the room. Clothes, books, pens and paper were scattered untidily across the surfaces and the bed was unmade. In contrast, Madame Lapointe was neat and tidy in a long, grey woollen jacket and skirt. Her short hair was tucked behind her ears and she looked pale. Lottie gave her the dress and Madame Lapointe returned Lottie's mask. 'Thank you for your kind gesture last night,' she said. 'I was able to enjoy the evening until... well, you know what happened. The poor colonel, such a sweet man. I can't stop thinking about it.'

'Me neither.'

'And now I've been told to speak to that Commissario Romeo again. He's an incredibly annoying man.' She ran a hand through her hair.

Lottie decided not to antagonise her by mentioning she'd told him about Madame Lapointe's dance with the colonel. 'Yes, he is,' she said. 'Very annoying.'

'And why has he come back to this hotel?'

'I suppose it's because Colonel Pickering was staying here, as was Signor Moretti. Commissario Romeo must be assuming the two murders are linked.'

'Perhaps they are, but I don't see how he needs to waste his time speaking to me.'

Madame Lapointe had been seen with both men shortly before they'd died. Lottie realised she could be a strong suspect.

The Frenchwoman stepped over to a velvet chair, moved some clothes out of the way, and sat down. 'So much for an enjoyable break in Venice. And to think I came here to escape everything.'

'Escape?'

'Yes, just some trivial things.' She gave a dismissive wave of her hand. 'Nothing too terrible, but I needed some time to myself and some space to write. I even asked the hotel for a writing table!' She pointed to an oak desk by the window which was piled with clutter. 'But I've been in no mood to do it. Anyway, I mustn't detain you any longer. No doubt Mrs Moore will need you for an errand of some sort. I don't envy you, Lottie, it's a demanding job running around after someone else.'

'I don't mind it too much. And if I wasn't doing this job, then I wouldn't have had the opportunity to see Venice.'

'I suppose not. It's a shame your stay hasn't been quieter.' Camille Lapointe's hands fidgeted in her lap and she gazed towards the window, as if distracted.

Lottie made her way to the door. 'Hopefully, I won't be needing to borrow any more of your dresses for the rest of our stay.'

'Oh, I don't mind,' said the Frenchwoman. 'It's nice to see them being worn. I always travel with too much. I can't possibly wear them all myself.'

'Well, thank you all the same and good luck with the commissario, Madame Lapointe.'

'Ugh, I shall need it.' She bit her lip, then turned to Lottie. 'Call me Camille, by the way.'

LOTTIE TOOK Rosetta out for a walk. 'Now I can call her Camille,' she said to the dog, feeling a little flattered. 'We may even become friends. Although I'm not sure I want to be friends with her if she murdered the opera singer and the colonel. Do you think she could have done something like that? She seems very uneasy this morning. Something you would expect, perhaps, from a murderer who doesn't want to be found out.'

Billy called over to her from one of the tables in the piazza. 'Isn't it awful?' he said as she approached. 'Two people dead! And I knew both of them! I never dreamt such a thing was possible. And here in Venice too!'

'It's sad indeed,' said Lottie, taking a seat.

Billy summoned the waiter, ordered two espressos, then mopped his brow. 'I simply don't understand it, Lottie, do you? Who's doing this? And why? The poor colonel. I didn't get to speak to him much at the ball last night, but I caught sight of him dancing with various ladies, including yourself, Lottie. He seemed to be having the time of his life! How lovely for an old man because there can't be a great deal of joy to be had when you get to that age, can there? You'd have thought that someone saw something, wouldn't you? Who was he with?'

'I know he was planning to dance with Camille Lapointe,' said Lottie. 'But I can't imagine she would have caused him any harm.'

'She's not the friendliest of people, but that's just her manner. Being unfriendly doesn't make you a murderer, does it?'

'She's actually a little friendlier once you get to know her.'

'Is she? Very well, I shall reserve judgement for the time being.' He patted Rosetta on the head. 'Poor Rosetta.' He pushed his lower lip out in sympathy. 'She must be missing her daddy very much. It's wonderful that you've taken her on and that Mrs Moore doesn't mind.'

'I haven't taken her on for good, I'm just looking after her for the time being. But I think Mrs Moore is assuming I've found someone else to look after her.'

'Oh golly, that's awkward. Good luck with it.'

The waiter brought over their espressos, and Billy knocked his back. 'I should get back to the hotel and start packing.'

Lottie gasped. 'You're leaving?'

'I'm afraid so.' He adjusted his black bow tie. 'I received a telegram from my friend in Rome asking when I would be arriving. Given all the unpleasantness that's occurred here, I thought now would be as good a time as any to make the journey. I realise that Commissario Romeo may wish to speak with me again.'

'You've spoken to him?'

'Yes, a number of times. Haven't we all?'

'Yes, we have.'

'I've given that funny deputy chap of his the address I'll be staying at, just in case he needs me for anything. I'm breaking the train journey by stopping off at Bologna, so I'll be staying there this evening and will arrive in Rome tomorrow.'

'Well that's a shame.'

'I'm half-sad to leave and half-not. I've met some lovely people here though, such as yourself.'

'Thank you. I think Mrs Moore has plans to visit Rome, perhaps we can meet you there?'

'Yes! That would be wonderful. Other than my old school friend, I don't know anybody else there. If you can persuade Mrs Moore to visit, that would be smashing.'

'I'd like that.' Lottie sipped her espresso and enjoyed its rich, bitter flavour.

'Now, before I go and do my packing,' said Billy. 'I've been meaning to ask you about someone. I know I shouldn't say it and she's a lovely lady, but...' He lowered his voice and leant in. 'Don't you think that there's something a little bit funny about Jane Harris?'

'I hadn't noticed.'

'I've come across her a couple of times now in places where you wouldn't expect her to be.'

'Such as where?'

'Outside a jeweller's shop on the Rialto Bridge yesterday morning. Quite early, at a time when you don't expect to see many people about.'

'Perhaps she thought the same of you?'

He gave a chuckle. 'I hadn't thought of that. However, I also saw her earlier and where do you suppose she was?'

'I don't know.'

'In a street next to the Palazzo Sacrati, the very place the ball was held last night!'

'Did you speak to her?'

'Oh yes.'

'And did she explain what she was doing there?'

'She told me she was paying her respects to the colonel.'

'There doesn't seem to be much suspicious about that.'

'Perhaps not.'

'But why were you there?'

He laughed. 'Oh, I realise what this looks like. I'm popping up in unexpected places too! I was actually visiting a barber's shop.' He ran a hand over his dark, oiled hair. 'Do you like?'

'It looks very nice.'

'Thank you.'

Could Jane Harris be suspicious? Lottie wasn't convinced. 'I don't see how a lady of Jane Harris's age could fatally wield a dagger and a sword,' she said.

'It could be tricky. But let's not fall into the trap of under-estimating someone just because they're over seventy. Sometimes in the heat of the moment, people can find extraordinary strength.'

'And push Signor Moretti over the balustrade of a balcony?'

'Possibly.' Billy gave a nod as he considered this. 'Perhaps I'm being a bit silly about Jane Harris. There's just something a little bit shifty about her and I can't put my finger on it.'

'Investigators have to consider all possibilities.'

'And I'm no investigator! As you can probably tell. I'd be hopeless at it! I shall leave it to the police and the commissario, he seems like a safe pair of hands.'

'If you say so.' Lottie finished her coffee, avoiding the silty bit at the bottom of the cup. 'Do you know who I have suspicions about?'

'Who?'

'The man dressed as the plague doctor. Did you see him at the ball?'

'Yes I did. Scary costume, isn't it?'

'And a scary man. I noticed him staring at me.'

'Oh no, that's not nice.'

'And I saw him leave early, around the time the colonel was murdered. In fact, he could have carried out the attack and fled immediately.'

Billy's eyes widened. 'Really?'

'I've told Commissario Romeo about it, but he doesn't seem very interested.'

'That plague doctor chap needs to be properly investigated.'

'Especially if he's also the dog snatcher.'

'Of course! He wears the same mask, doesn't he? It must be the same man. I don't know what it is about Venice, but they need to sort out their law and order here. It's blatantly the man dressed as a plague doctor who's causing all this bother! Oh, Lottie, what can be done to find him?'

'I don't know. I'd like to think of something.'

'And I'd like to help, but I'm not terribly clever, I'm afraid.'

'Nonsense! I'm sure you are.'

'Nope. I'm not clever at all. On the other hand, Lottie

Sprigg, I think you're very clever indeed. With a little bit of work, I think you're capable of tracking that man down.'

'Do you think so?'

'Oh yes. You should get onto it. I can tell you're good at this sort of thing.'

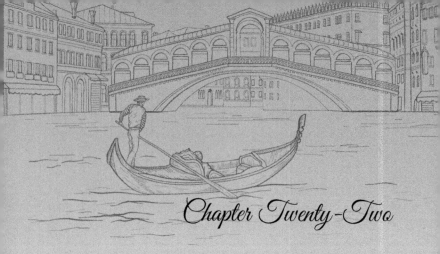

Chapter Twenty-Two

'AT WHAT TIME did you dance with Colonel Pickering last night?' Commissario Romeo asked Camille Lapointe.

They sat in the lounge. She tried to appear as nonchalant as ever, smoothing her dark woollen skirt and sucking on her silver cigarette holder. But it wasn't easy. His grey eyes kept a steady contact with hers and she worried he could see the things she wasn't telling him. 'I don't know what time it was,' she said. 'I wasn't wearing a watch.'

'Was there a clock in the ballroom?'

'I didn't see one.'

'You must have a rough idea of the time. Beginning of the evening? Middle? Or the end?'

'Close to the end of the evening, it wasn't long before... well, you know what happened. Perhaps the dance with me was his last dance. I don't know.'

'When did you last see him?'

'When we parted ways on the dancefloor.'

'And where did he go after that?'

'I can't tell you for sure, but he said he was going to get a drink. The drinks were being served in the salon, so that must have been the reason he went there.'

'And where did you go after your dance?'

'I remained in the ballroom and danced with a delightful gentleman from Verona.'

'And after that dance?'

'I chose not to dance the next one, and it was cut short anyway once the news of the colonel's death spread.'

'So where did you go after your dance with the man from Verona?'

'I went to the powder room.'

'Did you go into the salon?'

'No.'

'Did the colonel mention anyone he was going to meet or speak to?'

'No.'

'And what did you talk about during the dance?'

'My hometown of Biarritz. He had visited it in the past.'

'Did he mention anyone he had fallen out with or disagreed with? Anyone who would have borne him any animosity?'

'No, nothing. If he had told me anything useful at all, Commissario, then I would pass it on to you.'

'Are you sure about that?'

'Quite sure.' His eyes didn't move from her face. Why couldn't he look away for just a moment? She stared back. 'Why do you doubt me?'

'I don't doubt you, I'm just not sure whether you're telling me everything.'

He sat back in his chair and surveyed her as he inhaled on his thin little cigarette. 'Tell me about your husband, Madame Lapointe.'

Her heart sank into her stomach. She smoothed her hair but she knew she was struggling to hide her unease. 'My husband is none of your business, Commissario Romeo. I could just as well ask you about your wife.'

'Except my wife isn't a criminal.'

'Neither was my husband!'

'You are no longer married?'

'No.'

He gave a nod. 'So Monsieur Vincent Lapointe is your former husband.'

'Vincent? No, you're quite wrong there, Commissario.'

She couldn't give away any signs that she was bothered by the mention of his name. She breathed as slowly as she could. Not only would it calm her, but it would also show the commissario that she was completely unbothered by his talk.

'What was your husband's name?'

'I don't have to tell you that, it's irrelevant.'

He gave a sniff and asked his bespectacled deputy for some papers. The deputy handed them to him and he leafed through them. Camille wished she could read what was on them, but he held them in such a way to make it impossible. 'I had our records checked,' he said, 'and Monsieur Vincent Lapointe was a member of a gang involved in a bank robbery eight years ago. He and his accomplices were arrested, and he is currently serving time in prison in Paris. He was arrested here in Venice, Madame Lapointe.'

She shrugged. 'I've never heard of him.'

'We don't come across many people with the surname Lapointe in Venice.'

'Well, we do in France. I can only imagine this man you mention is someone who shares the same surname and nothing more.' She fixed him with her gaze.

'So you're telling me that Vincent Lapointe is not your former husband?'

'Absolutely.'

'And what will he say if I ask him about you?'

'He will have no idea who I am.' This was a lie and she could only hope he wouldn't check. The commissario had two murders to solve, surely he wouldn't waste his time trying to prove a link between her and Vincent Lapointe? She suspected he was trying to use the information to unsettle her and make her tell him something.

She had to ensure his plan wouldn't work.

Chapter Twenty-Three

AFTER CHECKING on Mrs Moore and finding her asleep, Lottie made herself comfortable in the lounge with her notebook. She'd sat as far away from Commissario Romeo as possible. She'd spotted him speaking to Camille Lapointe and now the Frenchwoman had just left the room. She had left swiftly, as if keen to get away. Lottie wondered what the commissario had asked her. And why did she seem nervous?

Bearing in mind Billy's words of encouragement, Lottie opened her notebook and wrote:

April 3rd

4.00 pm – I met Amadeo Moretti in the hotel after I found Rosetta

7.00 pm – we went to the opera, I saw Camille Lapointe leaving Amadeo Moretti's dressing room (she still hasn't admitted it was her).

10.00 pm – dinner with Amadeo Moretti. Joined by Jane Harris and William Cecil-Raikes. Amadeo Moretti went to have drinks with Colonel Pickering at the bar.

11.45 pm - Colonel Pickering went to Amadeo Moretti's

room to look at war medals. He left ten minutes later. Witnessed by maid?

Midnight – I heard shouting while on the balcony of Mrs Moore's room.

Between midnight and 1.00 am on April 4th – Amadeo Moretti murdered.

APRIL 4TH

9.30am – I met Colonel Pickering by the canal near the hotel, he dropped some money.

7.00 pm – we went to the ball. Met Colonel Pickering, Jane Harris, William Cecil-Raikes and Camille Lapointe.

9.30 pm (approx.) – I danced with Colonel Pickering then gave my mask to Camille Lapointe in the powder room.

9.55 pm (approx.) – I saw the man in the plague doctor's costume leave the ball.

10.00 pm – Colonel Pickering was discovered murdered in the salon.

LOTTIE CHEWED on the end of her pen while she considered what other information she should write down. Was there anything she'd missed? Her thoughts were interrupted as Jane Harris approached. She wore a pale linen dress and held her pink sun hat in one hand. The old lady sank into a chair and patted Rosetta on the head. 'You have a good vantage point from here, Lottie,' she said. 'You can see exactly who's coming and going. Dreadful news about Colonel Pickering isn't it? What is the world coming to?'

'I wish I knew.'

'Me too. The police seem to be concentrating their investigation on this hotel. There must be some clues in Colonel Pickering's room.'

'Such as what?' said Lottie.

'I don't know. Letters perhaps? Diaries? Maybe there's evidence of someone else having been in the room.'

'Such as who?'

'I don't know. I'm only guessing. But it's important to understand as much as possible about the colonel's character and conduct. From that, the police can develop some theories on who would have wished to kill him and why.'

Jane appeared to be giving a lot of thought to the investigation. Lottie showed her the timeline she'd written in her notebook. Jane put on her spectacles and examined it. 'Oh, I like this! Very interesting indeed.'

'I'm not sure what it tells us though.'

'Nothing immediate perhaps. But it's a good way to organise the information and, maybe if we sit here and absorb it for a little while, some fresh ideas might emerge.'

'Have you got any theories?' Lottie asked.

'Secrets,' she said. 'The things people try to hide. Now I know the colonel had some secrets.'

'What were they?'

'That would be telling. I'm trying to determine if they're relevant to his death. If they're irrelevant, then it wouldn't do to tell.'

'Why not?' said Lottie. 'He's no longer around.'

'Ah, but we don't know what family he has back home, do we? I know he was a widower, and he was very much in love with his wife. The grief caused him to make some unwise choices. But if I tell everybody everything I know, and it gets back to his family, well, they might be distressed by it. Particularly if it has nothing to do with his death. One has to be very careful with the information one comes by, he could have children who might be upset by it.'

'Was he caught up in something?'

'There was something, but I'm not sure yet how serious it was or whether it had anything to do with his death.'

'I know about the money.'

Jane's eyebrows lifted. 'You do?'

'Yes. If that's what you're referring to.'

'Well... it has something to do with it. How do you know about the money?'

'He dropped some of it and I helped him pick it up.'

Jane chuckled. 'Silly old fool. Well, at least it was you helping him and no one else.'

'So you know about the money too? He asked me not to mention it to anyone.'

'That doesn't surprise me.'

'So what was he up to?'

'My dear, I shall tell all when I can be sure it's safe to do so.'

'Will you tell the police what you know?'

'Yes. I don't know a great deal, mind you. And it might not be relevant.'

Lottie gritted her teeth with impatience. She wanted to tell Jane that she could be trusted not to tell anyone else the colonel's secret, but Jane seemed the sort of lady who wouldn't be persuaded.

'What about Signor Moretti?' said Lottie. 'Did he have a secret?'

'From what I hear, quite a few.' She checked her watch. 'Oh, I need to go. It was nice talking to you, Lottie. I shall see you later.'

Lottie watched the old lady exit the lounge. Although she was a little bent with age, she could move at a brisk pace.

Mindful of Billy mentioning that Jane Harris kept popping up in unexpected places, Lottie felt an urge to follow her. She folded up her notebook. 'Come on Rosetta, it's time for another walk,' she said.

· · ·

They exited the hotel just in time to see Jane leaving the far corner of the sunny piazza. Lottie pulled her sun hat on and set off after her, nursing a pang of guilt. Was it wrong to follow an old lady who might be doing little more than enjoying a stroll? Having just had a conversation with Jane, secretly following her felt deceitful.

As Lottie and Rosetta turned into a street, she saw Jane Harris's unmistakable pink hat up ahead. The old lady had checked her watch before leaving, did that mean she had to be somewhere by a certain time?

Rosetta kept stopping to sniff at various things along the way. Lottie tugged gently, yet firmly, on the lead. 'Come along we don't want to lose Jane.'

They left the busier streets and Lottie had to hang back more, just in case Jane turned and saw them. Lottie soon felt lost. She looked up at the sun to establish which direction they were heading in. 'East I think, Rosetta,' she said. 'Actually, perhaps it's south? Oh I should practise this skill, I'm sure it would come in very handy.'

Jane's pace slowed as they entered a small square. Jane checked her watch, then looked in the windows of a few shops. She spent some time outside a jeweller. Lottie hid with Rosetta behind an ice cream cart at the far corner of the square.

She watched as Jane checked her watch again, then crossed to another corner of the square and disappeared down a narrow alley.

'Come on Rosetta!' Lottie hurried after her.

As they turned into the alley, Lottie was dismayed to discover it ended at a canal. In the shadowy gloom, all she could see was Jane's silhouette. If Jane turned around now, she would see Lottie and her dog. Hurriedly, Lottie returned to the square and positioned herself so she could peer around the corner into the alley. Jane stopped and looked up and down the canal as if waiting for someone. Moments later, a gondola drew up in front of her.

'Did she arrange the gondola?' Lottie whispered to Rosetta. 'Or did it just turn up? She kept checking her watch so I think she must have arranged it. But why here? Why couldn't she have just walked to the Grand Canal to find one?'

Jane was talking to the gondolier about thirty yards away, but she hadn't got into the boat. The gondolier looked familiar. Lottie squinted so she could discern his features a little better, he had a long face and appeared to have dark hair beneath his boater hat. 'I think it's Vito!' whispered Lottie. 'Jane must have arranged to meet him here! But why?' She watched as Jane climbed into the gondola and sat down. Then Vito pushed away with his foot, dipped the oar into the water and they were gone. 'Where are they going?' Lottie looked down at the dog. 'And what are you eating?'

Whatever it was, Rosetta had now consumed it and was licking her lips. 'Come on, let's see if we can follow the canal.' Lottie glanced around the square and saw a passageway leading off in the direction in which the gondola had travelled.

'Come on Rosetta!' She jogged over to the passageway, turned into it, and was relieved to see a little bridge up ahead. She slowed her pace as she reached the bridge and pulled the brim of her hat over her face to shield her features. She stepped up onto the bridge and cautiously glanced to her right in the direction of the gondola. It was about twenty yards away, clearly marked by Jane's pink hat. Lottie ducked down behind the wall of the bridge, worried the occupants of the gondola might see her. Their voices carried across the water but Lottie couldn't hear what they were saying. Once she felt sure the gondola had passed beneath the bridge, Lottie carefully stood and peered over the other side to watch them continue along the canal. There was no path alongside this section of canal and there was a sharp turn to the right at the end.

'It's going to be difficult to follow them,' she said to Rosetta. She continued over the bridge and looked for a turn that would take her left on a route parallel to the canal and then hopefully join it after its right turn.

It was a while before she found a turn to the left and, frustratingly, the street then bent sharply to the right. 'Here we are in the maze of Venice again, Rosetta.'

Lottie took turns left and right, hoping that she would find herself close to the canal again. Finally she found a street leading to a bridge. She jogged to it as quickly as Rosetta would allow and cautiously surveyed the gondolas on the water. There was no sign of Jane's pink hat.

Lottie sighed. 'I think we've lost them Rosetta, time to go back.' She wasn't sure where she was, all she could do was retrace her steps and hope she could find somewhere familiar.

Billy had been right, Jane Harris appeared to be up to something. 'Why didn't she tell me she was going on a gondola ride?' she said to Rosetta. 'You'd have thought she might have mentioned it when she spoke to us at the hotel. Did she simply forget to mention it? Or did she deliberately hide it?'

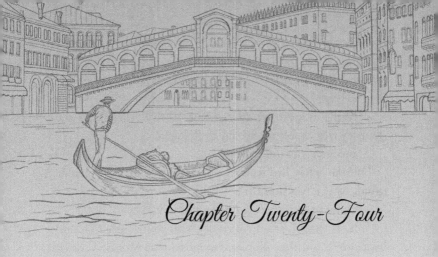

Chapter Twenty-Four

THE STONE BALUSTRADE of the balcony was warm beneath Billy's hands, and the sunlight on the canal dazzled his eyes. It was a shame to be leaving, but his trip to Venice hadn't been what he'd expected at all.

'Mr Cecil-Raikes?' In response, he returned to his room where Stefano, the bellboy, stood next to a luggage trolley loaded with cases. 'Everything is packed for you, signor,' he said.

'Thank you, young man.' Billy put his hand in his pocket and gave Stefano a twenty centesimi coin.

'Thank you! That's very generous of you, signor! If you're ready, then I'll take the luggage down to the lobby.'

Billy gave a final glance around the room. 'Yes, I'm quite ready, Stefano. Thank you.'

The bellboy opened the door and wheeled the trolley out of the room.

'How do you take the trolley down the stairs?' Billy asked. 'There's no elevator in this old building, is there?'

'I wheel it to the top of the stairs and then carry the cases down, I'm quite used to it.' He smiled. 'Where are you travelling to next?'

'Rome is next on the agenda. I shall break the train journey with an overnight stay in Bologna.'

'Bologna is a beautiful city.'

'From what I've seen of your country so far, Stefano, I think every city is beautiful.'

'Quite true. Although Naples not so much.'

'Now that's just a bit of rivalry with your southern friends, is it not? I must see Naples, I want to visit Mount Vesuvius! And that poor little place which was buried under all the ash and lava. What's that called again?'

'Pompeii? Or perhaps you mean Herculaneum?'

'Yes, those places. They need to be visited and, afterwards, I shall take the boat over to Sicily.'

'I wish you a safe journey on your travels, signor.'

'Thank you. You're a good lad, Stefano, and you work hard. I hope the manager, Signor Borelli, realises that one day.'

'Thank you, Mr Cecil-Raikes.'

'I know some guests are extremely appreciative of you, though.'

'Which ones?'

'That young girl, Lottie, is rather fond of you, wouldn't you say?'

Stefano's face went the colour of beetroot and Billy chuckled.

FIVE MINUTES LATER, Lottie walked into the hotel lobby with Rosetta and saw Billy with his pile of cases. 'Have a safe trip.' She forced a smile, sad that he was going. She found him enjoyable company. 'It's been lovely to meet you, Billy. It's a shame two tragedies occurred during our stay here.'

'Well, remember what I said earlier, Lottie? I think that, with your brains, you can help solve it.'

She laughed. 'I don't know about that.' Then she lowered her voice to a whisper. 'Although I have just seen Jane Harris doing something odd.'

His eyes widened. 'Is that so? What did I tell you?'

'She appears to have secretly met a gondolier, and they went off together somewhere.'

'Intriguing. Well, good luck with it and hopefully we shall meet in Rome and you can tell me if you learn anything else. And if we don't manage to meet in Rome, then ask Mrs Moore to look me up on your return to England. I plan to be back there by the end of the summer.'

'I will do. We'll see you again soon, Billy.'

Stefano approached and gave Lottie a smile before turning to Billy. 'We have a gondola ready for you, signor.' He picked up two of the cases.

'Marvellous!' said Billy with a grin. 'Let's go!'

LOTTIE WENT UP to the hotel room. She was just ushering Rosetta from the hallway into her little room when she heard Mrs Moore call out.

'Is that you, Lottie?' Her voice sounded weak.

'Yes.'

Lottie made sure Rosetta was hidden by the suitcases before stepping into the dingy room. 'Shall I open the shutters in here and let some air in?'

'Yes, that's a good idea.'

A bright shaft of light fell onto Mrs Moore's face.

'Oh heavens! That's bright.' She propped herself up into a sitting position. 'Were you talking to someone when you came in just then?'

'No.' Lottie must have whispered something to Rosetta, she hadn't realised she'd done it.

'That's odd, I could have sworn you were speaking to someone in a hushed voice. I thought it might be that bellboy.'

'Why him?' Lottie felt warmth in her cheeks.

'Because you like chatting to him and I couldn't think who else it could be. Never mind, I must have been imagining it.'

'I've just bumped into Billy,' said Lottie. 'He's just left for Rome. He sends his regards.'

'Billy's left? But I didn't even have the chance to say goodbye!'

Lottie was tempted to suggest that if she'd dragged herself out of bed, she might have found a chance. 'He says we can catch up with him in Rome.'

'Well, that's good, I should like to see him again. Although he'll probably have moved on by the time we end up there. We're off to Paris.'

'Paris? When?'

'Tomorrow.'

'Tomorrow?' Lottie felt her shoulders slump. She didn't want to leave Venice, not yet. She wanted to find out who was responsible for the murders. She couldn't possibly leave with the crimes unsolved.

'We're going to Paris because I did some detective work,' said Mrs Moore.

'Detective work?'

'Yes. I woke about an hour ago and called out for you before realising you weren't here. So I picked up the telephone and spoke to Lorenzo in reception and asked him to find out for me what Prince Manfred's next public engagement is. I had hoped he'd be attending another event here in Venice, but apparently he departs for Paris today.'

'So that's why we must go to Paris?'

'Why else? My plan was to dance with him at the ball last night and I missed my chance because the colonel was murdered. It's imperative that I'm at another party with him soon. Now what I need you to do, Lottie, is to speak to Lorenzo and get him to reserve a hotel in Paris. I should think Prince Manfred is staying at the Ritz, but it's unlikely they'll have space for us at such short notice. Failing that, Le Pavillon de la Reine or Le Meurice will do.'

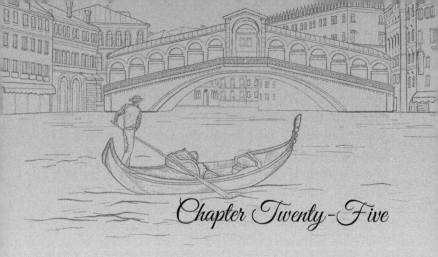

Chapter Twenty-Five

WITH A GLUM FACE, Lottie made her way to the hotel reception desk. She had to hope that Mrs Moore wouldn't discover Rosetta in her room. It was unlikely Mrs Moore would go into her little box room, but there was a risk Rosetta might let out a little bark if she was feeling bored. What was going to happen to Rosetta when they left for Paris? Lottie had no chance of keeping her secret anymore. And she couldn't bear the thought of parting with her. Everything seemed rather taxing all of a sudden.

As she waited for her turn at the reception desk, she pulled her notebook out of her bag and looked at the timeline she'd written that morning. She'd been close to both incidents. Surely there was a useful piece of detail she'd missed? But no matter how much she wracked her brains, she couldn't come up with anything new.

With a lump in her throat, Lottie asked Lorenzo to book a hotel in Paris, and he found space at Le Meurice. It was Mrs Moore's third choice, but it was probably an exceptional hotel all the same. Ordinarily, Lottie would have been excited about staying there.

Lottie bumped into Stefano once she'd finished at the reception desk. He was carrying a tall pile of parcels. 'What's happened?' he asked.

'Do I look that miserable?'

'Yes.'

'We're leaving for Paris tomorrow.'

'Oh?' The pile of parcels wobbled, and he had to steady the top one. 'You don't want to go?'

'I realise I can't stay here forever. But I would like to stay a little while longer.'

'I would like you to stay here a little while longer, too.'

'Would you?'

'Yes, I would. But anyway, it's the nature of hotels that people come and go. Paris is a beautiful place.'

'And so is Venice. If only I could stay here and find out who's behind the murders. And if only I could find that masked man who left the ball early and I could prove Commissario Romeo wrong!' She sighed. 'Or perhaps it's foolish of me to think I can do something about it. I found out quite a few things, but I'm no closer to working out who could have done it. I've just been reading some notes I made on everything.'

'You made some notes?'

'Yes. And I've realised we only have the colonel's word that he was in Amadeo Moretti's room for ten minutes. A maid saw him leave, I wonder if she knows exactly what time it was. Do you know if Commissario Romeo has spoken to her?'

'He must have done, he's spoken with all the staff here.'

'Maybe we can speak to her. The colonel said she had brown wavy hair and spectacles.'

'I'm not sure who that is, I'll ask around.'

'Hopefully we can speak to her before I leave tomorrow. And I don't know if she's a murderer, but Jane Harris is certainly up to something.'

'What's she up to?'

Lottie told him how she'd followed her and saw her meet the gondolier. 'The two of them seem a little suspicious,' she said. 'Billy saw her snooping around too. I think there's quite a lot she's not telling me.'

The parcels wobbled again. 'I'd better get these dropped off,' said Stefano.

'Alright. But if you can, keep a close eye on Jane Harris.'

CAMILLE LAPOINTE EMERGED from the lounge as Lottie was walking to the staircase. 'Hello Lottie,' she said. 'I walked past Billy's room, the door was open and the staff were cleaning it. He's left!'

'Yes, he has,' replied Lottie. 'He's gone to Rome.'

'Rome? That was rather sudden, he didn't even say good-bye. It makes you wonder, doesn't it?'

'Wonder what?'

'If he's running away from something. Perhaps he's responsible for the murders?'

'Billy? No, he couldn't be.' But Lottie thought about this, could Camille be right?

'Come for a quick walk with me.' Camille took her arm. 'There's something I need to tell you. If I tell you, then you can tell Mrs Moore and then everyone will know about it.' Camille had clearly realised Mrs Moore was a gossip.

'What is it?'

They crossed the lobby and stepped out into the piazza. It was late afternoon now, and the sunlight was a pleasant golden glow. Camille turned down the side of the hotel and they walked to the canal and the place where Lottie had seen Colonel Pickering drop his money.

'Commissario Romeo has found out something about me,' said Camille. 'And he's going to use it against me.'

'That's not very nice.'

'If everybody else knows about it, then the commissario no longer has the power. Does that make sense?'

'I think so.'

Camille lit a cigarette, and they strolled alongside the canal. 'I was once married to a gentleman called Vincent Lapointe. I was young and naive when we met, and I fell madly in love. I had a strict upbringing, I was educated by nuns in a prestigious school on a hill outside Lourdes. I couldn't wait to leave and, when I did, I headed for the bright lights of Paris. I was desperate to get away from school, as you can imagine.'

Lottie pictured a remote, strict school run by fearsome nuns and nodded in agreement.

'In Paris I found work as an assistant to a couturier. A dressmaker is what you English call it. It sounds glamorous but really I was just a bonne à tout faire. You know what that is? The person who does all the jobs no one else wants to do. I had to tidy up after everyone else, deliver messages and that sort of thing. But the boutique was on the Champs-Élysées. What better place is there to be in Paris than that?'

'Even I've heard of it,' said Lottie.

'It's a wonderful place. And it was in a bar close to there that I met handsome Vincent Lapointe. I did not know about men, so I didn't realise how shallow his charm was. We married in a tiny chapel and I didn't even tell my family! I suppose I thought I was being rebellious. We had a nice lifestyle, Vincent had a beautiful apartment in the 8th arrondissement. He gave me money to dress myself well and have my hair done just so. We dined out in all the best restaurants, and Vincent knew everybody. I didn't have to work for the couturier anymore, it was my dream to be a writer and he told me I could do that. I spent my time writing ideas in pretty notebooks and sipping coffee in gorgeous cafes.'

'It sounds like the perfect lifestyle,' said Lottie.

'It does, doesn't it? Too good to be true, perhaps. Vincent went out a lot, and he didn't always tell me where or who he was meeting. He told me it was business. After a while, I felt lonely, and I grew unhappy. The more I challenged him, the angrier he got. He didn't like me questioning him about anything. After a while, I wondered if I could leave him. And just as I was thinking about it, there was a big bank robbery in Paris. Five million francs were stolen. That was the last time I saw Vincent. He came home all in a fluster and began packing his bags. I didn't know what had happened, and I was worried about questioning him because of his temper, but I pleaded with him not to go. He told me he would telephone me and that I was not to worry. He gave me a kiss and then he was gone. The next day, the police arrived and arrested me.'

'Arrested *you*? But you had nothing to do with it!'

'Exactly. They didn't believe me when I told them I knew nothing about what he had done. Eventually, they released me when they could see that I was just a young woman who did not know what he had been up to. It was a horrible time. I had no idea about the man I had married! It horrified me when I discovered he had been involved with a bank robbery.'

They reached a bridge.

'Let's go left here,' said Camille. 'There is a place close by which sells very good ice creams.'

'So what did you do next?' Lottie asked.

'Nobody felt sorry for me, of course. Why would they? In their eyes, I was just as bad as my husband. How could I not have known what he was up to? So I moved to Biarritz and from there I tried to start a new life. There was quite a lot of money in the bank account that he never claimed, nor did the police ever enquire about it. I realise now that it was probably stolen from somewhere, but I had nothing else to live on and I didn't know how to return it to anyone. So I've been using it as my own account ever since.'

'Did the police ever catch your husband?'

'He was arrested here in Venice a few months after the robbery.'

'Here?'

'Yes. I don't know what he was doing here, but at his trial in Paris, they talked of how he knew several criminals in various countries. After the robbery, he was busy trying to hide the money they took. He's now in prison in Paris. I didn't go to his trial but I read about it in the newspapers. And now Commissario Romeo has discovered my history. He's realised I've been trying to hide it.'

'Why did you hide it?'

'Because of the shame. If people find out I was married to a criminal, then they will assume I'm just as bad. It's not the sort of thing you can ever mention, is it?'

'No. Perhaps you could have changed your name?'

'Yes, I realise now that perhaps it would have been best to do so. I thought about it but I didn't want to revert to my maiden name because it was Chofleur.'

'What's wrong with that? I think it's a nice name.'

'In French it means cauliflower.'

'Oh.'

'I like the surname Lapointe, I think it is a good surname for a writer. And, despite everything that has happened, I am quite traditional at heart. I remain married and so I still bear his name. And perhaps there is nothing so disgraceful about the secret after all? I know that I've done nothing wrong.'

Lottie thought about the story of Signor Moretti's past. He'd been a criminal too. 'It's very interesting to hear about your estranged husband,' she said. 'And I don't think there should be any shame if you've done nothing wrong. But there's something you haven't yet explained.'

'What? I've told you everything.'

'Not quite. You haven't yet admitted that you visited Signor Moretti in his dressing room.'

'Oh, that.' She blew out a cloud of smoke. 'Yes, I lied about that too because there is a connection with my husband. Amadeo Moretti once visited us in Paris. He saw me at the hotel a few days ago and it was quite a shock. We didn't speak on that occasion, but I wanted to visit him to make sure that he would keep our association secret. He agreed, of course, he was a very amenable man. I liked him. In fact, he reminded me of my husband a little. But Amadeo's criminal lifestyle got the better of him, I feel sure that his killer was someone out for revenge. I couldn't tell you who, but that really is all I know.'

They stopped outside a small shop with a sign saying "Gelato" and numerous pots of colourful ice cream in the window. 'Now then,' said Camille. 'Which flavour would you like? The strawberry is very good.'

Lottie wondered why Camille had poured her heart out to her. Was it really because she wanted everybody to know about her past so it couldn't be used against her? Or was she creating a story to cover the actual truth?

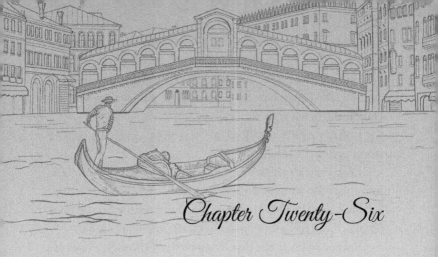

Chapter Twenty-Six

'I SUPPOSE LE MEURICE WILL DO,' said Mrs Moore when Lottie returned to the hotel room. Her employer was wearing her silk Japanese print robe again and had wrapped her hair up in a yellow scarf. 'I shall write to Prince Manfred to inform him that's where we're staying.'

'Does he know who you are?'

'Does he know who I am? What an impertinent question, Lottie! Of course he does. We met last summer at Somerset House in London.'

'I didn't mean to be impertinent. He must meet so many people on his travels that it must be difficult for him to remember.'

'I'd like to think I'm more memorable than most people.'

'Yes, Mrs Moore, I think you are.'

'Good.' She glanced around the room, hands on hips. 'Now I think we need to make a start on our packing, there's a lot to do. I'll fetch one of the cases from your room.' To Lottie's horror, she began striding towards her room, where Rosetta was currently hiding.

'I can do it!' said Lottie, dashing ahead of her.

'Well, if you insist, but I'm perfectly capable of fetching a case myself. I may have had a headache all day, but I'm not completely helpless.'

Lottie opened the door to her room, and Mrs Moore stood right behind her.

Lottie's heart thudded in her ears. She was going to come into the room with her and see Rosetta!

She turned to her employer, her hand resting on the door handle. 'I can fetch it for you and take it into your room.'

'I want to select the case. I want one of the bigger ones for my bulky items.'

'Oh.'

'Is something wrong?'

'No! I'll just get one of the bigger cases.'

'Are you trying to stop me from going in there?'

'No, not at all.'

'Then let me through! Anyone would think you had something to hide in here.'

'Such as what?'

'I don't know. That bellboy perhaps.'

'Why does everyone keep mentioning him?'

'Because we see you having your secret little chats, that's why. I suppose it's only natural that you get on well with him, it's not often you meet people your own age in these places. Now let me choose a case.'

There was nothing more Lottie could do. She gave a slow exhale and moved aside to let Mrs Moore pass, preparing herself for the hysterical reaction.

Her mouth was dry.

She followed Mrs Moore, scanning the room for Rosetta. She spotted her beneath the bed, her corgi nose protruding from beneath the eiderdown. *Stay there*, she silently willed the dog.

Mrs Moore picked up a case. 'This one's quite large,' she said, 'but I think there's a larger one somewhere.'

Lottie felt sick. If Rosetta made a move, then Mrs Moore would spot her immediately. 'This one?' she suggested, desperate to hurry things along.

'Yes, that's a good size, isn't it? But is it the largest?'

'Yes,' said Lottie through gritted teeth.

'I thought there was a larger one.'

'No, this is it.'

'Are you sure you're alright, Lottie? Something seems to be bothering you.'

'I'm fine.' She forced a smile.

'What are you looking at?'

'Nothing.'

'You keep looking at the floor over here.' Mrs Moore turned in the direction of the bed. Lottie felt dizzy, she was sure she would faint. And if she fainted, then Rosetta was bound to come running out from her hiding place and lick her face.

'Shall I take this case into your bedroom?' she asked. It took all the energy she had to overcome her light-headedness.

'Yes, alright then. If you're sure that's the largest.'

Mrs Moore stepped past her and returned to her room. Lottie breathed out a large sigh of relief and followed her employer with the case.

Her problem wasn't over though. How was she going to take Rosetta to Paris? It was going to be impossible.

Mrs Moore flung open the doors of her wardrobe. 'Did I really bring this much with me? I haven't even worn half of it yet.' She sighed. 'Actually I'm hungry, I've just realised I haven't eaten all day. Let's go down to the restaurant.'

≈

'It's quiet in here this evening,' said Mrs Moore, glancing around at the empty tables. She had changed into a black silk dress. 'Where is everybody?'

'I suppose they're not in the mood for socialising after the colonel's murder.'

'I suppose not. Surely they still need to eat, though?'

They sat at the same table they had dined at with Amadeo Moretti. Lottie couldn't help glancing at the place where he'd sat and at the little hooks on the wall where the fearsome medieval weapons had hung. It was discomforting.

The food arrived quickly because the restaurant was so quiet. 'So what have I missed today?' asked Mrs Moore as she tucked into a plate of pasta in anchovy sauce.

'Quite a lot.' Lottie recalled her conversation with Camille Lapointe. 'I have some gossip for you.'

'Gossip? Where from? The bellboy?'

'No, not him. I had a conversation with Madame Lapointe, we're on quite friendly terms now.'

'Are you? Well, that's some achievement, she's not exactly the friendliest person I've met.'

Mrs Moore listened intently while Lottie told her Camille's story. By the time she'd finished, she realised it was probably the longest Mrs Moore had gone without interrupting.

'Well, that's fascinating!' she said. 'I always knew there was a whiff of scandal about the woman.'

'But please don't tell anybody,' said Lottie, hoping this instruction would encourage Mrs Moore to share the supposedly secret story.

'My lips are sealed.' Lottie knew they wouldn't be. Mrs Moore continued, 'it's quite astonishing how naive some women can be, don't you think? Fancy not realising she was married to a criminal!'

'She admits she was naive, she grew up in a convent on a mountain top.'

'A mountain?'

'Well, a hill outside Lourdes.'

Mrs Moore took a gulp of wine. 'That's no excuse, I'm afraid. I believe most women are born with good instincts.'

Lottie chose not to mention Mrs Moore's three failed marriages and took another mouthful of pasta instead.

'Did I tell you about the merchant I danced with at the masquerade ball?' said Mrs Moore. 'Signor... Mancini... Medici? Marzini... oh, I can't remember. Anyway, he told me about his daughter who's run off with a circus performer. Can you believe it? A very wealthy family and he spent a lot on her education.'

Lottie listened to Mrs Moore's story about the merchant's daughter and the circus performer as she finished her pasta. As she ate, she noticed Stefano loitering by the restaurant door. He caught her eye.

'And by that stage, they'd bought three chimpanzees,' continued Mrs Moore. 'Who are you looking at, Lottie?'

'I think Stefano wants to speak to me about something.'

'Stefano?'

'The bellboy.'

'Oh him, yes, I expect he does. Signor Borelli needs to keep a close eye on that boy. Now where was I?'

'Three chimpanzees.'

'That's right. And can you believe they all lived in the same caravan? Mr Marzini, Mancini, what's-his-name, told me he had to stop visiting them because... What now?'

Stefano had approached the table.

'Excuse me, signora, I'm terribly sorry for interrupting. I need to have a word with Miss Sprigg about the arrangements for your departure tomorrow.'

'Do you?'

'Yes. We don't want a, er... repeat of the incident when you arrived.'

'When I fell into the canal, you mean?'

'Er... yes.'

'No, we certainly don't want that happening again! Although why arrangements must be discussed now, I don't know.' She gave Lottie a dismissive wave. 'Go and sort out what you need to sort out. I can tell you the rest of the story on the train tomorrow, we shall be on it all day.' She picked up her drink. 'I shall see if there's anyone to talk to in the lounge.'

Lottie joined Stefano and followed him across the lobby.

'Has something happened?' she asked in a hushed tone.

'Jane Harris left the hotel a few minutes ago. Didn't you ask me to keep an eye on her?'

'Yes.'

'So let's go.'

'Don't you have work to do? You'll get into trouble.'

He gave her a grin. 'I finished at eight o'clock.'

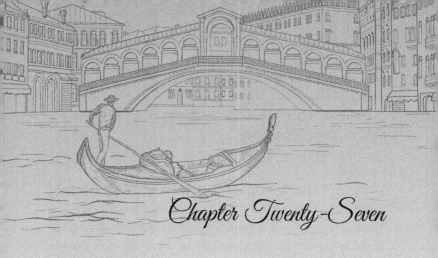

Chapter Twenty-Seven

LOTTIE AND STEFANO stepped out into the warm evening air. It was dark and lights glimmered in the cafe and restaurant windows.

'I saw her crossing the square,' said Stefano. 'I think she was heading for the street on the right. Let's go!'

They ran across the square and turned into the street. It was busy with people looking for places to eat. Ten yards ahead, they could see Jane Harris walking briskly away from them. As it was the evening, she was without her pink sun hat. Instead, Lottie focussed on her distinctive grey hair tied in a bun at the nape of her neck.

'I wonder what she's up to?' said Lottie.

'Hopefully we will find out.' Despite having finished his shift, Stefano still wore his red, braided bellboy uniform, and he attracted a few glances as they walked.

They followed Jane Harris as she turned left and right, then left and right again. 'How does she know her way around so well?' said Lottie. 'Once again, I'm lost.'

'And some of these streets are dark and quiet,' said

Stefano. 'I can't say that I would want to be walking along them on my own.'

'I don't know where she's leading us, but I think it's different from this morning.'

They turned into the next street and suddenly Jane had vanished.

'What?' said Stefano, running on ahead. Lottie followed, and they reached a canal. 'She must be in that gondola,' said Stefano, pointing to a boat which was moving away from them. It was a dark silhouette on the water, lit with a single lamp.

'What can we do now?' said Lottie.

'It's simple. We find a boat.'

'We can't just take one!'

'Yes we can. They're moored for the night and no one will want to use them again until the morning. I know who owns that one.' Stefano pointed to a little rowboat tethered to a post by a doorway. 'It belongs to Ferdinando Alessi, he owns a trattoria here and is a good friend of my uncle. Everyone knows each other in Venice.' He took off his jacket and stood there in his shirt sleeves. 'Can you hold my jacket while I fetch it?'

'What? You're going to swim?'

'It's only five yards.'

'You can't!'

'Yes, I can. I've done this sort of thing lots of times before.'

He lowered himself into the water, gasped at the cold, then reached the rowboat in a few powerful swimming strokes. Lottie watched as he hauled himself into the boat, untied it, and picked up the oars. Moments later, he was alongside her, beckoning her in.

'But you can't just take someone's boat!'

'Ferdinando won't mind!'

Lottie cautiously climbed in and perched on the little wooden plank which served as a seat.

148

'Are you ready?' Through the gloom, Lottie saw a large grin on Stefano's face. He was clearly enjoying himself.

'As ready as I'll ever be,' she said, gripping the sides. Her voice echoed in the narrow canal.

Stefano began to row and Lottie turned on her seat so she could look ahead. The gloomy canal appeared to fork and she could just make out the light of the gondola moving away from them.

'It's turned right,' she said, impressed with the speed they were moving at. 'You're good at rowing, by the way.'

'Of course I am. I'm Venetian!'

'Why is Jane Harris going for a gondola ride in the evening?'

'Some people like to do it. The canals have a certain atmosphere at night.'

'A creepy atmosphere I'd say.' She gave a shiver and looked up at the dark stone walls looming either side of them. Lights glimmered at some windows, but other buildings were in darkness. She didn't like the dark water doors at the sides of the canal. Something - or someone - could lurk there unseen.

The gondola ahead moved to the left of the canal and then appeared to stop altogether, just in front of a bridge.

'Now we can catch up with them,' said Stefano. The boat rocked as he rowed faster, the splash of the oars echoing in the narrow canal. 'We can't let them out of our sights.'

But the faster they moved, the quicker the boat ahead seemed to travel. Now and again, Lottie saw the dark form of the gondolier pass across the light, but she couldn't see the passenger at all.

'Is Jane Harris even in the boat?' she said.

'She must be. Where else did she go?'

'I don't know. It's baffling.'

The gondola continued onwards. 'They're speeding up,' said Stefano. 'I need to row faster.'

The boat rocked even more.

'Careful!' said Lottie.

'I'm trying to be careful! But we need to catch them.'

The canal bent sharply to the left and Stefano was moving the boat at such a speed that he found it difficult to turn. The gondola ahead moved deftly around the bend. Frantically, Stefano turned the boat.

They passed a terrace where people sat at little tables by the water's edge, a few of them were peering at the boat ahead with interest.

'Why are they looking at the gondola?' said Lottie. 'It's as if they've seen something unusual.'

At the next bend, Lottie heard a shout. 'Oy!'

But Stefano was rowing too fast to respond to the warning call and suddenly they were in the path of a gondola coming towards them. The gondolier steered deftly around them and hurled a torrent of words which Lottie guessed were insults.

'Spiacente!' said Stefano. But the gondolier continued to shout even after they'd passed.

Stefano shouted something back, distracted. Lottie could barely see a thing in the dark.

Out of the gloom, brickwork loomed ahead.

'No!' cried out Lottie as the boat hit the wall with a thud and a horrifying splintering sound. There was a violent lurch to the left and, for a moment, Lottie thought she might stay in the boat. But her weight pulled her downwards, and she slipped into the water, gasping as the cold hit her stomach and chest.

She splashed about, trying to keep afloat.

'I've got you,' said Stefano's voice in her ear. 'Just keep still.'

He held her just below her armpits. 'We'll be fine, can you swim?'

'Yes.'

'I think I can see a doorway. We can swim to it. Are you alright if I let go of you?'

'I think so.'

'Follow me.'

She could only just see him, and he was heading for the darkest part of the wall. Lottie didn't want to go there, but she knew she had to get out of the water.

Her clothes and shoes were heavy as she swam, and the cold made her emit large gasps.

'There are steps here,' echoed Stefano's voice ahead of her. She followed him and soon found her footing on some slimy stone steps.

Stefano was out of the water already. 'Here's my hand,' he said, helping her out.

Lottie could barely see a thing now.

'There should be a door here,' he said. She heard the turn of a handle, then the creak of hinges.

'It's open!' he said.

'Is it someone's house?'

'It must be.'

'We can't go in there!'

'What do you suggest?'

'Nothing. I suppose we have to do it.'

The door opened into darkness, Stefano took Lottie's hand and she stumbled after him. 'There are steps here,' he said. She felt for them with her feet and carefully climbed them, her teeth chattering with the cold.

There was light beneath the door at the top of the steps. It opened out into a hallway with a red and gold rug on a marble floor. On one side was a staircase and on the other was a wide door, which Lottie hoped would offer them an escape. There appeared to be no one about.

Lottie held her breath as she followed Stefano to the door.

Then she startled as she heard a shriek behind her. She turned to see a maid, her mouth open in horror.

'Bueno sera!' said Stefano as he pulled open the main door and they scurried through and out into the street. They ran as fast as they could until they reached the end.

'Told you it would be fine,' said Stefano as he caught his breath. He ran a hand through his wet hair and wrung out the tail of his shirt. Lottie's dress clung to her, and she shivered. She was as wet as Mrs Moore on the day of her arrival in Venice.

'I suppose my jacket is still in the boat?' said Stefano.

'I'm afraid so. It's most likely in the canal now.'

'I can come back tomorrow and fish it out. Now let's get back to the canal, we might be able to find out who's on that boat.'

'How do you know the way?'

'I'm just guessing.'

He took her hand again and led her down a couple of streets before a bridge came into view. 'Is this the same canal?' asked Lottie.

'I think so. And if we're lucky, we've got just ahead of them now.'

They ran up onto the bridge and looked up and down. The canal was in darkness, but then Lottie spotted a faint light. 'There!' She pointed at it, even though her hand was barely visible.

They listened to the steady splash of the oar in the water, and the dark silhouette became more discernible.

'I don't think there's a passenger in it,' said Stefano. 'Where's Jane Harris?'

'I don't know.'

As the gondola drew closer, they realised there was some-thing unusual about the gondolier. From his outline, Lottie could see he was wearing a cape and, in the dim evening light, there was something about his features which made her shudder. Then she stifled a scream as she saw how malformed his pale white features were.

She wasn't looking at a man's face. She was looking at the plague doctor mask.

'Oh no.' Her knees went weak.

'Ferma!' called out Stefano.

But the figure ignored him, and the gondola passed beneath the bridge.

'We need to find out who this man is.' Stefano leapt to the other side of the bridge and hoisted himself onto the wall.

'Careful, Stefano!'

He didn't reply. Instead, he slid away, disappearing completely into the dark.

Then there was a loud thud.

Lottie looked over the wall, desperate to see the outcome.

In the lamplight of the gondola, Stefano and the gondolier were grappling with each other. Stefano appeared to be pulling at the mask and the gondola was rocking from side to side and turning widthways across the canal. A few angry words were exchanged in Italian and then the two men became locked in a scuffle. The gondola rocked some more and the pair toppled into the water with a loud splash.

For the third time that evening, Stefano was in the canal. Lottie could see something white in his hand, it was the plague doctor's mask.

Now they would discover his identity.

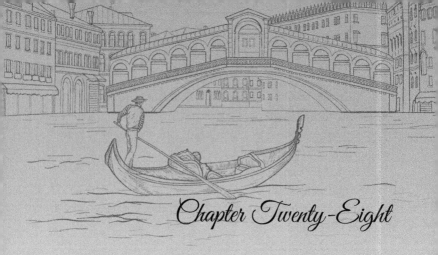

Chapter Twenty-Eight

'WHAT ARE YOU TWO DOING?' asked Vito Lombardo, as he stood dripping by the side of the canal. He'd pulled off his wet cape and held the plague doctor mask in his hand.

'We could ask the same of you,' said Lottie. She felt wary of him. Could he be a murderer?

'Why are you dressed up like this?' Stefano asked Vito. 'You've been scaring people!'

'There is only one person I want to scare,' said Vito. 'The dog snatcher.'

'But people think you are the dog snatcher!'

'I know, and it wasn't my intention.'

'Have you found him?'

'No.'

'Where's Jane Harris?'

'Out on patrol near the Piazza San Marco. She's been helping me.'

Lottie tried to comprehend this. 'Jane Harris has been helping you find the dog snatcher? How did she know you were looking for him?'

'We were both doing it separately, but we kept encountering each other and so we decided to do it together.'

Stefano shook his head. 'This is getting stranger and stranger.'

'So do you know who killed Signor Moretti and Colonel Pickering?' Lottie asked Vito.

'No.'

'Were you at the ball last night?'

'Yes, I was.'

'Dressed in this costume?'

'Yes. I've always enjoyed dressing up as Dottore Peste.'

'Why?' said Lottie. 'It's a scary costume. Are you the person I saw leaving the ball early last night?'

'Yes, I left early. My wife wanted me to be home by eleven o'clock.'

'Your wife didn't want to go to the ball?' asked Lottie.

'No, she doesn't like that sort of thing.'

Could he be believed? Lottie wasn't sure.

'You should have stopped when we called out to you,' said Stefano. 'Then we wouldn't have fallen into the canal.'

'We fell into the canal because you jumped into my boat! And I didn't want to stop because I was worried what you might do to me. There's been a lot of talk about the masked figure.'

'What do you expect?' said Stefano. 'If you want to find the dog snatcher, then you should do it without a costume.'

'I didn't want to be recognised. I wanted to find the dog snatcher, but I didn't want him to know who I was.'

Vito's reasons for dressing as the plague doctor seemed rather flimsy to Lottie. Either he was fibbing or he was someone who enjoyed dressing up and frightening people.

'I don't think it's right that Jane Harris is wondering about Venice at night on her own,' said Lottie. 'Let's find her and escort her back to the hotel.'

'I don't think it's right either,' said Vito. 'But try talking to her, she won't listen to anyone.'

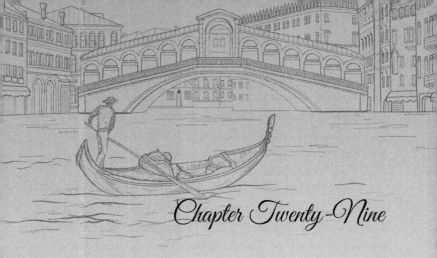

Chapter Twenty-Nine

'SO LET'S go over this again,' said Commissario Romeo. He rubbed a weary hand over his face, it was late in the evening. 'The lady came in here and asked to look at some diamonds?'

'That's right,' said the jeweller, Mario Ricci.

'And you willingly obliged?'

'I only willingly oblige once I've made a judgement about the customer, Commissario. I could see her clothes were expensive, and she wore some nice jewellery. She also knew what she was talking about, she was only interested in our one carat diamonds.'

'So you asked her to take a seat over there.' The commissario gestured at a plush velvet couch. 'And then you fetched the bag of diamonds and gave them to her to inspect?'

'Yes. I placed them on the table beneath the lamp there so she could examine them closely. She appeared to like them very much.'

'I think we know how much she liked them. Now it's the next bit which I need to understand. Once she had finished looking at the diamonds, she told you she would need some time to think about her purchase.'

'That's right. Each diamond was about one hundred thousand lire and she was interested in all five. It was quite understandable that she wished to think about it.'

'So you put them back into a little drawstring bag which she then picked up and put into her handbag.'

'That's right. It was an unusual move, and I just assumed she was being a little bit absent-minded. I immediately asked for the bag and she acted very embarrassed about it and was exceptionally apologetic. She took the bag out of her handbag and rested it back on the table again. Then she looked at her watch and seemed surprised. She said she had to hurry because she was late for a dinner appointment.'

'Which meant that she got out of your shop as quickly as possible.'

'Yes, it was quite hurried. After she had left, I took the bag out to the back of the shop, and it was only when I opened it that I saw there were five small pebbles in it instead of the diamonds.'

'And that's when you alerted your staff and you all ran about looking for her and couldn't find her anywhere. So you telephoned us.'

'That's right, Commissario. She has taken five hundred thousand lire worth of diamonds. I don't know how she managed to find a small bag identical to the one the diamonds were in, I can only guess she must have been in here scouting out the shop a few times before she carried out the act.'

'That's usually how these jewel thieves operate.'

'I've been so stupid! We'd been warned the jewel thief was believed to be in Venice. We were on the lookout for her, even though we had been told she was a master of disguise. She came across as such an innocent lady.'

'What was her nationality?'

'It's difficult to say. She spoke fluent Italian but, from her accent, I could tell that Italian wasn't her first language. I didn't ask her where she was from, I didn't wish to pry.'

'And the description you gave my men is as follows.' Commissario Romeo referred to a page in his notebook. 'She wore a long powder blue dress and a matching three-quarter length satin jacket. The dress had a white collar and a blue ribbon at the neck and she wore a wide-brimmed hat with flowers on it. She had dark, wavy collar-length hair, quite a lot of rouge and wore spectacles. She was between thirty and fifty years old. Can you be more precise about her age?'

'Not really,' said the jeweller.

'And this happened shortly before you closed the shop today. Just before six o'clock?'

'That's right. she can't have gone far.'

'If it's the international jewel thief, and I suspect it is, then she'll be staying at one of the hotels. I've already got my men calling at each one, starting with the more prestigious hotels to begin with. She's clearly a lady with fine tastes.'

'I don't hold out much hope,' said Mario Ricci. 'She's probably changed into another disguise now. And you must be extremely busy trying to find the murderer. That's more important than a careless jeweller, isn't it?'

'We try to solve every crime we are called to.'

'But your men are stretched, Commissario.'

'I can't deny it.'

'And if I were that jewel thief, then I would have taken a gondola straight to the railway station and be on a train out of here by now.'

Chapter Thirty

'I WISH we could find out who the dog snatcher is,' said Jane Harris as Lottie, Stefano and Vito walked with her back to the Grand Hotel Splendore. 'I can't bear the thought of those poor little dogs being stolen. People shouldn't be allowed to get away with these things! And with all the dreadful murders happening, I just knew that the police wouldn't have the time to investigate the dog snatcher.'

'Has there been a disappearance since the poodle was taken?' asked Lottie.

'No, that's still the most recent incident. I had a good look around the area as soon as I heard about it and you'd never believe it, but I think the dog snatcher has something to do with our hotel.'

'What makes you say that?'

'The day after the poodle was taken, I found a piece of paper lying in the street close to where the poodle was last seen. It was folded up very neatly, and that's why it caught my eye. It clearly wasn't something which had been scrunched up to be thrown away. Someone had used it as a reference.'

They paused beneath a lamppost as Jane Harris took the

piece of paper from her bag and opened it out. Lottie recognised it immediately.

'X marks the spot very close to where the poodle was taken,' said Jane. 'And here, look, someone's drawn the route back to the hotel.'

'This is a map I used, Jane,' said Lottie.

'You?' She stared at her, open-mouthed.

'Yes, I accidentally dropped it.'

'You're the dog snatcher?' asked Vito.

'No, of course not! But the X marks the chemist where I had to buy Stark's headache pills for Mrs Moore a few days ago. Lorenzo on the reception desk drew this map for me. If you don't believe me, we can check with him now.'

'I believe you alright,' said Jane. 'Well, I never! I thought it had to be something to do with the dog snatcher. I suppose I can't really explain why a dog snatcher would draw a map of where they took a dog from, but there we go. How silly I've been!'

'And from what I hear, the poodle was found yesterday,' said Stefano. 'Apparently, he turned up after everybody thought he had been snatched. He had just wandered off.'

'So no one took him?' asked Jane.

'I don't think so.'

'Can we be sure that there actually is a dog snatcher?' asked Lottie.

'Everybody has been talking about him for a few weeks,' said Vito.

'But has anyone actually seen him? Or did they just assume that you were the dog snatcher in your costume, Vito?'

'I don't know. Are you thinking now that the rumours were false, Lottie, and when people saw me trying to find the dog snatcher, they assumed I was him?'

'It sounds a bit like it. If someone's dog has been snatched, then obviously it's very serious. But I think it's possible that if the poodle returned home safely, then maybe the others did too.'

'Well, I could certainly look into that,' said Jane. 'I'd be thrilled to discover the dog snatcher never existed in the first place. What a twisted individual. Even worse than that murderer, I'd say.' She stopped and looked Lottie up and down, then the two men. 'I've just noticed something,' she said. 'Why are the three of you dripping wet?'

BACK AT THE HOTEL, Lottie said goodnight to the others and trudged wearily to her room. They seemed to have solved the mystery of the masked figure and discovered why Jane Harris was snooping around so suspiciously. But they'd got no closer to discovering who had murdered Amadeo Moretti and Colonel Pickering. And she was now feeling sure they never would.

She stepped into the little hallway between the rooms and saw her bedroom door was open.

'Is that you, Lottie?' came Mrs Moore's voice from her boudoir. 'That was a long discussion about the arrangements for our departure tomorrow.'

Lottie looked down at her sodden dress. How was she going to explain her appearance? And why was her bedroom door open? Had Rosetta got out?

She felt tired and couldn't think of anything clever to say. She decided to step into Mrs Moore's room and face the music.

Her employer had changed into her silk robe and was reclining on her bed. Someone else was reclining on her bed, too. But not a person.

A dog.

Lottie gasped.

Rosetta looked quite content having her back stroked by Mrs Moore. Her eyes were half-closed in relaxation.

'Erm, I can explain,' said Lottie.

'When were you going to tell me about her?' said Mrs Moore with a smile.

'I don't know. I'm planning to find someone else to look after her before we leave tomorrow.'

'And if you don't manage that?'

'Well, I suppose I would have to tell you about her. Only there's no need because it turns out that you've found her. I didn't tell you because I know you don't like dogs.'

'I do like dogs, I just don't think it's practical having one travelling with us.'

Lottie looked at Rosetta and felt a pang of deep sadness. She couldn't bear the thought of saying goodbye to her.

Mrs Moore tickled Rosetta's tummy. 'She likes this.'

'Yes, she does.' Mrs Moore and Rosetta seemed rather accustomed to one another.

'Did you know?' ventured Lottie.

'Of course I knew! You silly sausage. I heard you whispering to someone yesterday and couldn't work out who it was. I'm relieved it wasn't that bellboy. And then I went into your room and found Rosetta asleep in there so I realised you were struggling to give her away.'

'Why didn't you say anything?'

'I thought it would be fun to leave it and see how long it would take you to admit she was here! You held out for some time.'

Lottie laughed. 'I did. I was getting anxious about the situation. Thank you for being so understanding. I'll do what I can to find a new owner for her.'

'Oh nonsense.'

'What?'

'She can come with us.'

'Really?' Lottie gave a little jump of excitement.

'Of course. I think I'm almost as attached to Rosie now as you are. I keep calling her Rosie rather than Rosetta, it's become habit.'

'It's a lovely name. I think we should call her Rosie. It's a little shorter.'

'Rosie it is then.' Mrs Moore picked up her lorgnette and looked Lottie up and down. 'You look a bedraggled mess. What on earth have you been doing with that bellboy? You need to explain what you've been up to.'

Chapter Thirty-One

AFTER BREAKFAST THE FOLLOWING MORNING, Lottie and Mrs Moore began their packing. Rosie climbed into the open cases on the floor and generally got in their way. Lottie was relieved she no longer had to keep her secret and she felt overjoyed the corgi could travel with them now.

Stefano called at the door and offered to help. He wore a jacket that was a size too big for him, and Lottie wondered if Signor Borelli had been angry at him for losing his previous one.

'We need all the help we can get, young man,' said Mrs Moore. 'Although I think we probably know the real reason you're here.' She glanced from Stefano to Lottie and grinned. Lottie avoided looking at Stefano until the heat in her face had faded. 'Perhaps I can relax on the chaise longue while you young people get on with the packing?' Mrs Moore added.

'Of course,' said Stefano. 'And while we're packing, I can tell you about the robbery at my father's jewellery shop yesterday evening.'

'Oh no!'

'That's dreadful!' said Lottie. 'And to think he'd been worried about it happening, too!'

'He had. And she caught them out, even though they thought they were prepared for it.'

'What did she take?' asked Mrs Moore.

'Five diamonds.'

'Was she armed?'

'No, she used a clever sleight of hand. She swapped the bag of diamonds for an identical bag containing five small pebbles.'

Mrs Moore gasped. 'Shocking, but rather clever, too.'

'A small bag containing pebbles, you say?' said Lottie. She recalled the little bag Rosie had found in the corridor two days previously. Lottie had been intending to hand it in at the reception desk, but it had slipped her mind. After taking the bag out of her pocket, she'd put it in a drawer of her dressing table and forgotten about it. She went to her room to fetch it.

'Was the bag like this?' She returned to Mrs Moore's room, holding up the little bag so Stefano could see it.

'I don't know exactly what it looked like,' said Stefano. 'But where did you find that?'

'Rosie found it in the corridor on the first floor. I thought it was strange that it contained five little pebbles, but now I understand why.'

'It must have been dropped by the jewel thief!' said Mrs Moore. 'The jewel thief is in this hotel! What's wrong with this place? It attracts nothing but criminality.'

'You'll need to take the bag to Commissario Romeo,' said Stefano.

'I've just had a thought,' said Lottie. 'I found it just after I had visited... gosh, you don't suppose it could be, do you?'

'What?'

'I had just visited Camille Lapointe. This little bag was on the floor near her room.'

'Madame Lapointe a jewel thief?' said Mrs Moore. 'I can't say that surprises me at all. After all, she was married to a criminal. All that nonsense about her not knowing anything is exactly that. Nonsense.'

Lottie felt saddened by this. She'd wanted to believe her chat with Camille the previous day had been honest, but it was possible the Frenchwoman had been lying. It could have been little more than a story to cover her tracks.

THE LUGGAGE WAS STACKED UP, loaded onto a trolley, and then wheeled over to the staircase where Stefano carried the cases downstairs. Lottie insisted on helping. A short while later, the cases were in the lobby, awaiting departure.

Camille Lapointe appeared, dressed in a fashionable burgundy jacket and skirt. 'I'm sad to see you leave,' she said.

Lottie forced a smile, but it was difficult to meet Camille's eye when she suspected she was the jewel thief. It was tempting to show her the bag and ask her to explain herself, but Lottie decided that such a confrontation was best left to the police.

'What time is your train?' asked Camille.

'One o'clock.'

'Make sure you see me before you leave and I'll give you the names of some excellent restaurants in Paris. You'll have a wonderful time, I know it!' She flashed a smile which seemed genuine and Lottie felt guilty for suspecting her. Camille went on her way, and Lottie didn't know what to think.

'The jewel thief,' whispered Stefano. 'Brazen, isn't she?'

'We can't prove it completely. Someone else might have dropped that bag.'

'Perhaps.'

Lottie looked at the pile of luggage and spotted a case she didn't recognise. 'What's this one doing here?'

'It's not yours?'

She pulled it out from the pile and laid it on the floor. 'No it's not. It's that case you brought up to our room on the first day we were here. How did it get here?'

'I put it in the luggage room. I don't know how it's got mixed up with your belongings again.' Stefano went to the reception desk and spoke to Lorenzo.

'Mystery solved,' said Stefano when he returned. 'Lorenzo looked inside it and assumed it was Mrs Moore's case. He brought it out and put it with the others.'

'But the mystery isn't solved,' said Lottie. 'The owner of this case hasn't claimed it. Shall we look inside again?'

Stefano opened the case, and they saw, once again, the pair of large lilac buckled shoes. Lottie rummaged through the garish clothes. 'There must be something in here which tells us who this case belongs to.'

'I haven't looked through it in detail,' said Stefano. 'I just assumed the owner would claim it. There are lots of belongings inside.'

Lottie touched something soft, which she initially thought was a fur stole. But the fur seemed too long. She pulled out a dark, wavy-haired wig.

'Interesting,' said Stefano.

'And there are more wigs in here.' She pulled out one with fair straight hair and then another with grey hair. 'Why would someone wear a grey-haired wig?'

'Someone old?' suggested Stefano.

'But there's also a dark-haired one. That would give someone two very different appearances.'

'Perhaps that's what some people like to do.'

'Someone who likes to drastically change their appearance, perhaps?'

Lottie examined a pair of gold-rimmed spectacles. 'There's something funny about these.'

'What?'

'The lenses don't alter anything. Let me try them on.' Lottie did so.

'They suit you,' said Stefano.

'I can see perfectly.'

'That's good.'

'But don't you realise? It means the lenses are plain glass, they're not proper lenses at all.' She took them off. 'You try.'

Stefano put them on and looked about. 'Everything looks the same.'

'Exactly. The person who wears these doesn't actually need spectacles. They're a disguise!'

Lottie rummaged through the case again. 'Someone uses these outfits to disguise themselves. It explains why there's no luggage label on this case. They don't want its contents associated with them.'

'Which is maybe why they didn't enquire about it? It's been held in the luggage store, they could have claimed it at any time.'

'I think this case contains the jewel thief's disguises,' said Lottie. 'We know they've been in this hotel because I found that little bag of pebbles.'

'Madame Lapointe's case?' suggested Stefano.

'We can ask her. We're not accusing her of anything, all we're doing is asking her if she recognises these belongings.'

'I AM EXTREMELY OFFENDED that you think I would wear such dreadful clothes!' said Camille after Lottie and Stefano had carried the case up to her room. 'Who even wears things like that? It has to belong to an English person. Only the English have such poor taste.'

Lottie bit her tongue, choosing not to argue. It was no surprise that Camille was denying the case was hers.

If she was the jewel thief, then she wasn't going to admit it.

'And look at the size of those shoes!' said the French-woman, pointing at the lilac buckled footwear. 'They're twice the size of my feet!' Lottie looked at the dainty slippers Camille was wearing and had to agree.

She decided to show her the bag of pebbles and see how she reacted. 'What about this?' She pulled it out of her pocket and held it up. 'Do you recognise it?'

'No.' Lottie scrutinised her face, looking for a sign of deceit. Camille shrank back a little, clearly disconcerted. 'Why do you think these things are mine? Where did you find them?'

'Just lying about in the hotel,' said Stefano. 'We need to track down the rightful owner before they depart somewhere.'

'Well, they're not mine. I wish you luck with it.'

'WHAT DO YOU THINK?' Lottie asked Stefano as they carried the case back down to the lobby. 'Do you think she was lying or not?'

'I don't know. I thought I'd be able to tell, but I can't. I think she looked uneasy.'

Lottie felt a snap of frustration. 'If only there was a better way of telling if someone is lying! I thought it would be easier than this.'

They set the case back down on the floor of the lobby.

'Right,' said Lottie. 'I'm going to take everything out of this and examine it in detail, there has to be a clue in here somewhere.'

Signor Borelli strode past. 'Stefano!' He appeared to ask what the bellboy was doing but Stefano had an answer which placated him. After a further exchange, he strode off again. 'I don't have long,' said Stefano to Lottie.

She pulled out each item and laid it on the floor next to the case. All the colourful jackets, skirts, dresses, wigs, spectacles, stockings and shoes. Stefano chuckled.

'What's so funny?'

'Madame Lapointe saying this case must belong to an English person because only the English dress so badly.'

'We can't all be fashionable French ladies.'

'No. But even so, you have to admit some of these outfits are quite bad.'

'Because someone has used them for dressing up in. They're not someone's real wardrobe. Wait a moment. What's this?'

In a bottom corner of the case was a piece of paper scrunched up so small that it was barely noticeable. Lottie picked it up, held the little ball in her fingers, and carefully used her thumbnails to prise it open without tearing it. Eventually, she could smooth it out and read it.

'It's a receipt,' she said. 'Booth and Hawkins' Gentlemen's Outfitters on Jermyn Street, London.'

'So they are English?'

'Three bow ties purchased at the end of February. Bow ties... There's only one English person I've seen here this week wearing bow ties. Oh no... you do realise who that is, don't you? Billy.'

They held each other's gaze as they tried to comprehend this.

'No, it can't be,' said Stefano. 'Mr Cecil-Raikes left for Rome yesterday and the jewel thief struck last night.'

'How do you know he left for Rome?'

'Well, I helped him pack and load everything into the gondola, and off he went to the railway station.'

'How do you know he went to the railway station?'

'He told me. But I suppose he could have been lying.'

'Perhaps he just went to another hotel here in Venice?'

'But, if it's him, he left all his disguises here.'

'Maybe he bought new ones? He probably realised that he'd mislaid his case, but he didn't want to claim it back because he was worried that people would have seen what was inside. He didn't want to be caught with a case of ladies' clothes.'

'It wouldn't be the first time. Some of our gentleman guests own cases of ladies' clothes.'

'That's their business, I suppose. But in this case, Billy didn't want to risk anything which could suggest he's the jewel thief. So he abandoned this case and must have bought himself some new outfits.'

'Perhaps he told the shopkeepers they were for his wife?'

'He could well have done. And perhaps he had another case of disguises too which he could use. It seems that Billy is a master of disguise. In fact, who is he? Is he even William Cecil-Raikes?'

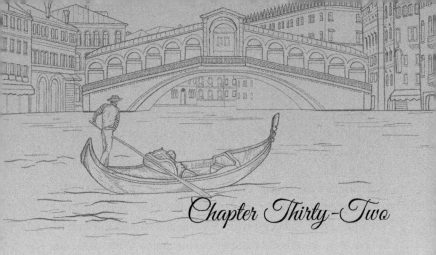

Chapter Thirty-Two

'WE NEED to tell Commissario Romeo what we've discovered,' said Lottie.

'But wait,' replied Stefano. 'Do we know for sure that we're right? It's a big accusation to make. We don't want to get it wrong and look foolish.'

'Who else could this case belong to?'

'I agree that the receipt from London for the bow ties suggests this case belongs to Billy, but that doesn't mean he's the jewel thief.'

'Why else would he have a case of ladies' clothing?'

'A private reason which he doesn't wish to disclose?' He gave a snigger, then recovered himself. 'Anyway, if the jewel thief was Billy disguised as a woman, then I really think my father would have realised it.'

'Can you be absolutely sure about that? The jewel thief is said to be a master of disguise, remember? Billy is clean-shaven and, with a wig, makeup, spectacles and a big hat and the clothes, perhaps he can pass for a woman?'

'And the voice?'

'He's not got a particularly deep voice. And besides, some women have a deep voice.'

'I suppose if my father saw a woman come into the shop, then perhaps he didn't feel the need to doubt she was a woman unless there was something obvious about it. But I'm still not convinced.'

'Alright then.' Lottie took a breath. 'Before we speak to the commissario, let's see if we can do a bit more work on this.' She pulled her notebook from her bag and flicked through it. 'There are several outstanding items here. What was the colonel doing with that money? What secret did he have which Jane Harris didn't want to tell me? And here's another one, who was the maid Colonel Pickering saw outside Signor Moretti's room on the night the opera singer was murdered?'

'Which maid?'

'I mentioned her to you. The one with dark wavy hair and spectacles and you told me you didn't know who that was.'

'I remember now. I was supposed to find out who she is.'

'How many maids work in this hotel?'

'I don't know. About thirty.'

'Does one of them have dark, wavy hair and spectacles?'

'Dark wavy hair, yes. Spectacles, yes. But the two of them together? I can't think who that is.'

Lottie glanced down at the case. 'What if it was Billy?'

Stefano's eyes widened. 'You think Billy disguised himself as a maid?'

'He could have done. If he's fooled a number of jewellers now, including your father, then he could easily have fooled someone passing him in the corridor late that evening.'

'But where did he get the uniform from?'

'Stole it? Has a maid's uniform gone missing from here in the past week?'

'I don't know.'

'I think you need to speak to your colleagues and find out.

Ask them if there's a maid matching the description of the maid who the colonel saw that night. And ask them if any uniform is missing.'

'Alright then.' He scratched the back of his neck.

'What's wrong?'

'You're being a little bit bossy at the moment.'

'That's because I need to be, our train leaves in a couple of hours. We could have this solved by then, Stefano!'

Chapter Thirty-Three

'LOTTIE!' chimed a voice across the lobby.

It was Mrs Moore. She wore a long, blue travelling dress and was accompanied by Rosie.

'You've told her about the dog?' whispered Stefano.

'Sort of.'

'I've just found three drawers with things still in them,' said Mrs Moore. 'Can you pack them for me, please? I'm going to take Rosie out for a little walk, she could do with some fresh air. As could I.'

'Enjoy your walk, Mrs Moore.'

They watched her go on her way.

'I shall ask around about the maid and the uniform,' said Stefano. 'I'll let you know what I find out.'

LOTTIE TOOK one of the cases back to the hotel room, hoping she could cram the remaining items into it. The drawers contained stockings and countless pairs of gloves, which she hadn't seen Mrs Moore wear since they'd left England.

Billy.

Could he really be the jewel thief?

Lottie pondered this as she balled up stockings and gloves and pushed them into every little space she could find.

Billy was such enjoyable, easy company. She'd warmed to him from the moment she'd first met him. Could he really be so deceitful? Although she couldn't prove it yet, she felt betrayed.

Could he also be a murderer? She recalled his words when they'd had an espresso together at the cafe in the piazza, *You should get onto it. I can tell you're good at this sort of thing.*

By encouraging her to investigate, he'd presumably hoped she wouldn't suspect him. He'd been attempting to call her bluff. How deceitful! His words had flattered her at the time, but now she realised how foolish she'd been. He'd been playing a game all along. He thought he was cleverer than her.

But now she'd show him.

STEFANO ALMOST CRASHED into her on the staircase as she carried the case down to the lobby.

'You're right!' he hissed with excitement. 'Nobody knows who the maid could be and two uniforms went missing from the laundry cupboard earlier this week!'

'Brilliant! Billy must have stolen those uniforms. Now he can't be in Rome if he committed the jewellery theft yesterday evening. He must still be here in Venice. But where? He could be anywhere!'

'Presumably he went to another hotel.'

'Did he ever mention another hotel to you which he liked?'

'No. Did he mention one to you?'

'No. But never mind, we can tell Commissario Romeo what we know. Have you seen him today?'

'No. Perhaps he's at my father's shop again.'

'I'll go there now. I think I have time.'

'I can't come with you, I have to work.' Stefano began giving Lottie directions but a new idea caught her.

'Wait, Stefano. Canaletto.'

'What about him?'

'Billy showed me a little book of Canaletto prints and he told me one of them was the same as the view from a hotel he liked.'

'What was it called?'

'I don't know! I don't think he said.'

'Which painting?'

'I don't know the name of it!'

'It could be anywhere!'

'Wait... it was a picture of a large church. How well do you know Canaletto's paintings?'

'Quite well.'

'I think Billy said it was one of the largest churches in Venice... Paolo something.'

'Santi Giovanni e Paolo?'

'That's the one! Do you know where it is?'

'Yes, but it's going to take me a very long time to give you directions.' He glanced around. 'Let's go there now. Signor Borelli will be angry with me, but... well, who cares?'

'Are you sure?'

'Yes! Let's go!'

LOTTIE FOLLOWED Stefano as they ran through the maze of streets, squares and bridges to the church. Their journey took about ten minutes and Lottie felt her lungs were about to burst as they arrived breathless in the square in front of the church. The square overlooked a canal and Lottie recognised the scene from the picture Billy had shown her.

'The hotel must be there,' she said, pointing to a row of cream and terracotta buildings on the other side of the canal.

'And luckily there's a bridge here,' said Stefano, they ran over to it and took the steps two at a time.

Looking down from the bridge, Lottie caught sight of a gondola moored by one of the water doors. Suitcases were being loaded into it and then a man climbed in who looked familiar.

He looked like Billy but he wasn't Billy. His hair was bushy instead of oiled, and he wore a scruffy, pale linen suit with no sign of a bow tie.

'Is that him?' she said.

'Yes!'

'Billy!' she called out.

His face turned towards her but showed no sign of recognition. Then he turned away and spoke to the gondolier.

'He's going to get away!' she said.

Stefano called out to the gondolier but there was no response.

'I'll go into the hotel and ask them to telephone the police,' said Stefano. 'You stay here and watch where they go.'

Stefano dashed off and Lottie watched helplessly as Billy's gondola began to glide away. Perhaps she imagined it, but she felt sure that the scruffy, linen-suited figure gave her a little wave.

Chapter Thirty-Four

'OH, THERE YOU ARE,' said Mrs Moore when Lottie and Stefano arrived back at the lobby of the Grand Hotel Splendore. She stood with Jane Harris and Camille Lapointe and Rosie sat at her feet. 'We need to catch our train. Where have you been?'

'We tried to stop Billy,' said Lottie. 'But we were too late. Hopefully the police will get him. Stefano called them from a hotel.'

'The police?'

'They have fast boats,' said Stefano. 'I think they'll get him.'

'I hope so,' said Lottie. She felt tired and deflated. Their walk back to the hotel seemed to have taken forever.

'Billy?' said Mrs Moore. 'But he's in Rome! I don't understand!'

'Has Billy done something wrong?' asked Jane Harris.

'I think so,' said Lottie. 'But somehow we have to prove it.'

'What exactly are you accusing him of?' asked Mrs Moore. 'Don't tell me it's... oh, is this him now?'

They turned to see a scruffy, linen-suited figure being led

into the lobby, handcuffed with a police officer holding each arm. Lottie grinned with relief.

Commissario Romeo strode into the lobby. 'This man has just been resisting arrest so he must have done something wrong!' He turned to Stefano. 'Where's the suitcase you told my men about?'

'Just here.' The bellboy pointed at the case on the floor.

Lottie caught Billy's gaze. Was there a slight spark of regret in his eye? If there was, then it passed quickly. He said something in a language she didn't understand, then looked away.

He wasn't Billy at all. He was someone else.

Lottie felt her teeth clench.

'I want to speak to him a moment,' she said to Commissario Romeo.

'Alright, but be quick.'

'Billy,' said Lottie coldly, 'or whatever your real name is. We found your lost case. It contains your disguises and there's a receipt in there for three bow ties from Booth and Hawkins' Gentlemen's Outfitters on Jermyn Street, London. And I found a bag of small pebbles too, I think you probably meant to swap them for diamonds but accidentally dropped them. You were careless, and we found you out.'

He pushed out his lower lip and said nothing.

The commissario bent down to examine the contents of the case. 'Does this belong to you?' he asked Billy.

'I've never seen it before in my life,' he replied.

Lottie shook her head and fixed Billy with a stare. 'And to think that I liked and trusted you!' Her voice cracked and she blinked away the tears which threatened to build in her eyes.

'You made a mistake,' said Billy in accented English. 'But never mind. You're only young. You will learn.'

Lottie knew this was her chance to confront him. 'Not only are you a thief,' she said. 'But I think you're a murderer too.'

'Now just a moment!' said Commissario Romeo, getting to his feet. 'How have you got that idea?'

'Lottie,' warned Mrs Moore. 'Are you sure about this? It's a very serious accusation.'

'I think this man disguised himself as a maid on the night of Amadeo Moretti's murder,' said Lottie. 'Colonel Pickering encountered a maid when he left Signor Moretti's room shortly before the opera singer's murder. He told me the maid had spectacles and dark wavy hair. No maid in the Grand Hotel Splendore matches that description. And two maids' uniforms have been stolen. I think Colonel Pickering saw this man shortly before he murdered Signor Moretti.'

'Why would this man murder Amadeo Moretti?' asked the commissario.

'I can't be completely certain.'

'Oh.'

'But I can make a good guess. This man who called himself Billy came to Venice to plan a diamond robbery. But then I think he bumped into someone he'd met before.'

'Who?'

'Amadeo Moretti. He had a criminal past and I think Billy murdered him because Moretti recognised him. He could have scuppered his plans to steal diamonds.'

'This can only be a theory,' said Commissario Romeo. 'You don't have any proof.'

'Perhaps I don't. But what do you think, Billy? Am I close to the truth? I remember you telling me I was good at this sort of thing.'

He gave a sniff but said nothing.

Commissario Romeo scratched his temple. 'If this man murdered Amadeo Moretti, then why did he murder Colonel Pickering?'

'Maybe Colonel Pickering recognised Billy as the maid in

that corridor?' said Lottie. 'Despite Billy supposedly being a master of disguise.'

'If the colonel recognised him, then why didn't he tell us?' asked the commissario.

'I don't know for sure,' said Lottie. 'But I do know that the colonel had a large sum of money on him the following day. I think he could have persuaded Billy to buy his silence.'

Commissario Romeo turned to Billy. 'Is that what happened? Did he ask you for money in return for staying quiet about having seen you?'

Billy sneered then scratched at his chin. 'Yes he did. He was blackmailing me. The silly old coot thought he could get his hands on my money! The colonel had a dreadful gambling problem. He'd proudly show me his winnings, then he'd bank them before having to go back and withdraw them again to pay off his debts. What sort of existence is that?'

'A miserable one, that's for sure.' The commissario gave a nod, as if he knew this from experience.

'Colonel Pickering saw through your disguise,' said Lottie.

'And I don't know how! I can't tell you how many people I've fooled over the years. But the colonel? I don't know how he did it. But if he'd left me alone and not threatened blackmail, then he'd still be alive.'

'So you're admitting murder?' asked the commissario.

'I had no choice! The pair of them were going to turn me in.'

'You're admitting the murder of Signor Moretti too?'

'Yes. I went too far, I realise that now. I was desperate for my run of success to continue, and I didn't want a faded old opera singer to get in my way. He wanted money from me, too. Isn't it astonishing how greedy some people are?'

'So greedy they will steal diamonds,' said the commissario.

'I was very lucky to find that cinquedea on the hotel restaurant wall,' said Billy. 'It was perfect for the job! It fitted into the inside pocket of my jacket. I had hoped Signor Moretti would float a little further down the canal, but unfortunately, he remained quite close to the hotel. I'm quite lucky, I suppose, that no one actually saw me do it. It was certainly risky, but I almost got away with it. And to think I could have been on the train to Rome by now! But you put a stop to that Lottie Sprigg and your little bellboy friend.'

'We had to!' said Lottie. 'You murdered two people!'

'I didn't plan to! My hand was forced. I had to do what I could to survive. I couldn't leave them both to get away with it, could I? I'm not a cold-hearted killer, but if someone is in my way, then they will have to be removed.'

'It's interesting how men like you justify their barbaric actions,' said the commissario. 'Perhaps if you hadn't been living a life of crime in the first place, then people wouldn't get in your way.'

'I have no time for blackmailers!' said Billy.

'But robbery and murder is alright?' asked Lottie.

'Sometimes it can be justified.'

Commissario Romeo instructed his deputy to pick up the case. Then he turned to Lottie. 'We need to take this man to the police station now. Thank you, Signorina Sprigg, for all your help. You have surprised me with your abilities. You have an old head on young shoulders.'

'That doesn't sound like a compliment, Commissario Romeo, but I shall accept it as one all the same.'

'Well done, Lottie,' said Billy in the cut-glass English accent he'd used in the past. 'I wasn't wrong about you, was I? You're actually quite clever for a lowly orphan.'

His description of her stung.

Lottie wiped away a tear as she watched him leave.

Chapter Thirty-Five

'I DON'T BELIEVE IT,' said Mrs Moore. 'Please tell me it's not true! When we first met Billy, he told me we'd met before. He knew about my sister and Fortescue Manor.'

'I suspect he'd been listening in on our conversation with Amadeo Moretti,' said Lottie.

'Oh dear. Is my voice really that loud?'

Everyone was too polite to respond.

'How did this even come about?' said Mrs Moore. 'And what did you have to do with it, Lottie?'

'She solved it,' said Stefano.

'With a lot of help.' She gave him a grin.

Mrs Moore wiped her brow. 'You're going to have to tell me all about it on our train journey, Lottie. I don't know how you find the time to do these things. I'm quite amazed at what you found yourself caught up in. Are you telling me Billy made *everything* up?'

'Yes. He's just a ruthless criminal. He will stop at nothing. Hopefully Commissario Romeo will discover his true identity.'

'And to think I allowed that Billy character into my room!'

'Fortunately, we didn't pose any threat to him. But he murdered the ones who did.'

'Poor Signor Moretti,' said Jane Harris. 'I gather he was no angel, but he didn't deserve to die. And neither did the poor old colonel. I felt very sad for him when I saw him gambling all his money in the casino. I tried to warn him it would come to no good, he was associating with some people in there who I could tell were quite unsavoury. But he wasn't going to listen to a little old lady like me, was he?'

'I'm afraid not, Jane,' said Mrs Moore. 'And it's a shame to be leaving Venice, but I can't say I'm sorry about it under the present circumstances. We shall have to visit again when all this has blown over.'

Lottie turned to Stefano. 'I hope your father gets his diamonds back.'

'So do I. I shall tell him to pull the hair of everybody who comes into his shop.'

'Why would you suggest that?' asked Mrs Moore.

'To find out if they're wearing a wig.'

'Of course.'

Signor Borelli marched into the lobby, launching a torrent of words at Stefano. Mrs Moore stepped forward and stopped him. 'Can I just say, Signor Borelli, what a delightful young man your bellboy is. I've travelled the world and stayed in many different places and I've never encountered such a charming, helpful, hard-working young man as this one.'

Lottie watched the hotel manager's expression change from anger to delight. 'Is that so, Mrs Moore?'

'Absolutely. Are you paying him well?'

'Very well.'

'Good. Because if you aren't, I'm quite sure he'll soon be poached by one of your rivals.'

'I see. Thank you Mrs Moore.' He turned to the bellboy. 'And well done, Stefano.'

Lottie and Stefano exchanged a smile.

'Goodbye Lottie, young dear,' said Jane Harris, stepping forward. 'It was a delight to meet you and discuss a few theories with you. I think you're a better detective than I'll ever be.'

'Oh, I don't know about that Jane, you worked hard on the mystery of the dog snatcher.'

'But I didn't exactly solve anything, did I? And to think I put so much importance on a map the hotel receptionist drew for you!' She laughed. 'I think I should bow out of sleuthing. Working with young Vito was great fun though. If I were fifty years younger, I should like to court him!'

Camille Lapointe stepped forward and gave Lottie an embrace and a kiss on each cheek. 'I enjoyed your company,' she said. 'Good luck on the rest of your travels.'

'Thank you Camille, and you.'

'I've told Mrs Moore all about the best restaurants in Paris. And if you ever come to Biarritz, you must let me know!'

'We will.'

Stefano began picking up the cases and carrying them over to the steps which led down to the door at the canal.

Lottie picked up a case and walked alongside him.

'I shall miss you,' said Stefano, meeting her gaze. 'A lot.'

'I shall miss you, too. And I don't think I'm going to forget last night's escapade on the canal in a hurry.'

He laughed. 'It was fun, wasn't it? Promise me you'll write.'

'I promise. I'll write to you as soon as we reach Paris.'

'Oh no!' said Mrs Moore as soon as she set eyes on Vito in the gondola. 'Not him again!'

'I promise not to rock the boat this time,' said Vito with a grin.

Lottie helped Mrs Moore step cautiously in. Once she was seated, Lottie picked up Rosie. She turned to Stefano. His lips were pushed together and his brow furrowed.

'Thank you for all your help,' she said.

'I enjoyed it.'

'Come along, Lottie!' called out Mrs Moore. 'We don't want to miss our train!'

Lottie turned back to Stefano and felt a lump in her throat as she leaned forward and gave him a quick kiss on his cheek. His face went a deep red. 'Promise you'll write too?'

'I promise.'

Lottie gave him a wave, then stepped into the gondola.

'Well done,' said Mrs Moore. 'Now then, andiamo! Let's go!'

'Is that the first Italian word you've used since we got here, Mrs Moore?'

'Yes, I believe it is.'

THE END

Thank you

Thank you for reading *Murder in Venice*. I really hope you enjoyed it! Here are a few ways to stay in touch:

Join my mailing list and receive a FREE short story *Murder in Milan*:
marthabond.com/murder-in-milan

Like my brand new Facebook page:
facebook.com/marthabondauthor

A free Lottie Sprigg mystery

Find out what happens when Lottie, Rosie and Mrs Moore catch the train to Paris in this free mystery *Murder in Milan*!

Lottie and Mrs Moore are travelling from Venice to Paris when their journey is halted at Milan. A passenger has been poisoned and no one can resume their trip until the killer is caught. Trapped in a dismal hotel with her corgi sidekick, Lottie is handed a mysterious suitcase which could land her in trouble...

Events escalate with a second poisoning. Lottie must clear her name and find the killer before the trip is cancelled for good!

Visit my website to claim your free copy:
marthabond.com/murder-in-milan

Or scan the code on the following page:

Murder in Paris

Book 2 in the Lottie Sprigg Mystery Series!

Lottie Sprigg - travelling companion to a wealthy heiress - is whisked into fashionable society on arrival in Paris. But a dinner party hosted by the Lenoir family goes awry when a body's discovered in the drawing room.

Who did the deed? Having chanced upon some clues, budding sleuth Lottie tries to make sense of mysterious conversations and bare-faced lies. She's assisted by her trusty dog, Rosie, and the local delivery boy. But when a second body is found, her theories come undone.

A bicycle chase and a scare in Pere Lachaise cemetery complicate the case. Lottie receives a sinister warning to keep away. How can she uncover a secret which someone is so desperate to hide?

Get your copy by following this link: mybook.to/parismurder

·

Printed in Great Britain
by Amazon

31847744R00118